Mrs. Henry Wood

William Allair

Or, running away to sea

Mrs. Henry Wood

William Allair
Or, running away to sea

ISBN/EAN: 9783337424404

Printed in Europe, USA, Canada, Australia, Japan

Cover: Foto ©Andreas Hilbeck / pixelio.de

More available books at **www.hansebooks.com**

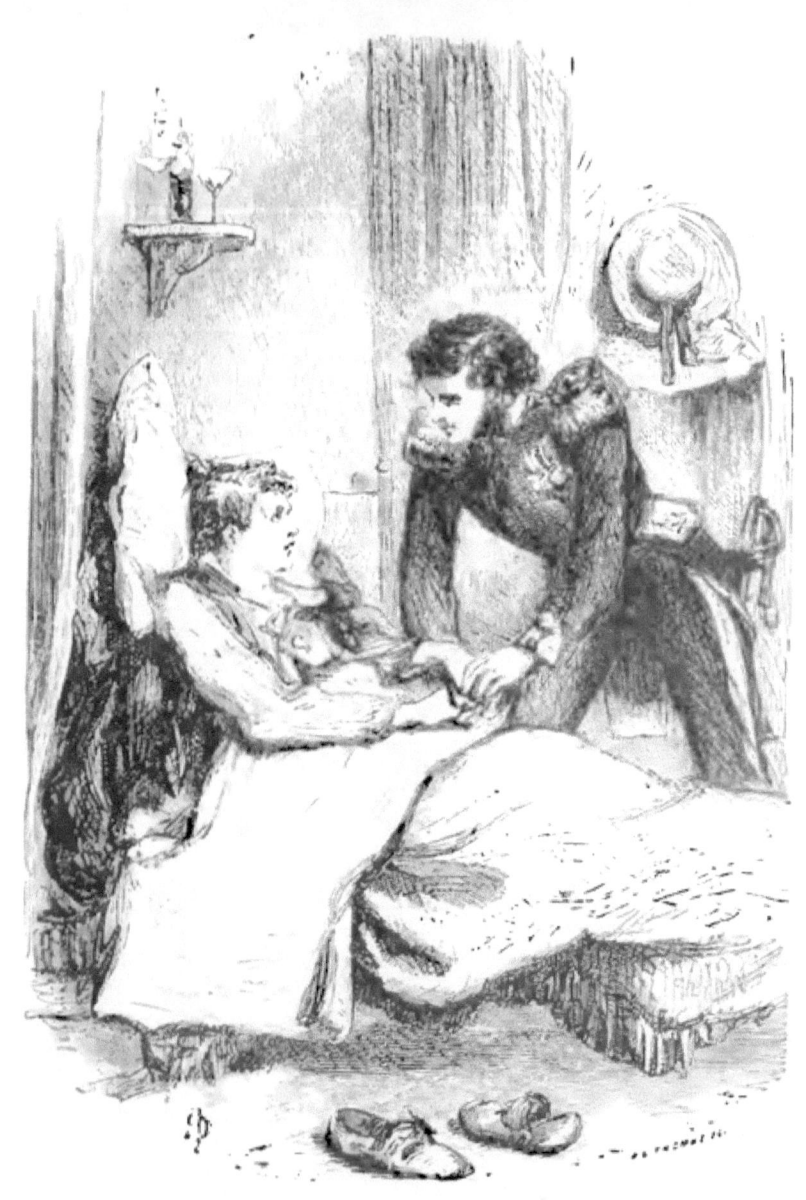

HARRY VANE'S INTERVIEW WITH WILLIAM ALLAIR.

Page 159.

OR,

RUNNING AWAY TO SEA.

BY

MRS HENRY WOOD,

AUTHOR OF "EAST LYNNE," "THE CHANNINGS," ETC., ETC.

FRONTISPIECE FROM A DRAWING BY F. GILBERT.

LONDON:

GRIFFITH AND FARRAN,

(SUCCESSORS TO NEWBERY AND HARRIS

CORNER OF ST PAUL'S CHURCHYARD.

MDCCCLXIV.

CONTENTS.

WILLIAM ALLAIR:

OR,

RUNNING AWAY TO SEA.

———————◆———

CHAPTER I.

THE TWENTY-NINTH OF MAY.

I LIKE writing for boys, and I am going to tell them a story of real life. I hope all those who are especially inclined to be scapegraces will learn it by heart.

Never was there a pleasanter village than that of Whittermead, situated in a charming nook of old England. It had its colony of gentlemen's houses, its clustering cottages, its farm homesteads. An aristocratic village it was pleased to call itself, and a loyal village, too; which was the cause, possibly, why sundry old-fashioned customs, that had become obsolete in most places, reigned there still in triumph. Its enemies were apt to ridicule the place, and reproach it as being, in reference to the world in general, "a day behind the fair."

Two days in the year were kept as public holidays, and Whittermead, in its ultra loyalty, prided itself upon the fact. The days were the twenty-ninth of May, and

A

the fifth of November. Had the show on the one day, and the Guy Fawkeses and fireworks on the other, been done away with, the boys would have broken out into open rebellion; more particularly, the scholars of Dr Robertson' school, a semi-public school of renown in the county. It is with the twenty-ninth of May that we have to do; but not a very recent one; I am telling you of years ago.

In the heart of the town there stood a white, detached house. It was inhabited by a gentleman of the name of Allair; a solicitor of good practice for a small local place. His eldest son, William, gives the title to this book.

On the morning spoken of, the church bells rang out a merry peal, heralding in the holiday; so early, that few people were awake to hear them. Their sound aroused many,—amongst others, William Allair. He started from his pillow, a good-looking, fair boy of fifteen, and stared around him.

"The bells already!" cried he, winking and blinking his blue eyes between sleep and wake. "And—if I don't believe it's a fine morning!"

Taking a flying leap from his bed, he pulled aside the window curtain, and the glorious beauty of a bright morning burst upon his delighted view—all the more beautiful from its contrast to many preceding days. The weather had been dull and gloomy up to the very last night, and bets were pending that the twenty-ninth would be the same. Boys ought not to bet; but they do: and I see no use to ignore the fact, when writing of them. It was a lovely landscape that met William's sight, as he looked forth; for this house of Mr Allair, built on a gentle eminence, commanded a view of the surrounding country. The blue sky, dark and serene, was without a cloud; the grass, fresh with the bright green of spring, glittered with dew drops; the hedges were gay with the white and pink-flowering May; the early birds were singing sweetly; and the many coloured flowers were opening to the morning sun. William Allair took it all in with greedy eyes, with a rapt movement of half-disbelieving delight.

"What a stupid I was, not to take Jenniker's bet that the day would be a bad one!"

He glanced at his watch, and found that it had stopped. In his flurry of anticipation the night before, he had forgotten to wind it up. Perhaps it was already late! Bursting out of the room with dismay at the thought, en chemise-de-nuit, as he was, he sprang across the corridor, and drummed sharply on the opposite door.

"Who's there? What is it?" cried a drowsy voice from the inside—that of his sister Alice.

He opened the door, and thrust in his head. "Now, you girls! Are you going to sleep all day? I knew what your boast was worth—that you'd be up first and call me."

"Is it late?" asked Alice, turning her head upon the pillow: while a pretty little face beside her rose up and stared.

"I am afraid it is. I forgot to wind up my watch. Of course! that's sure to be the case—the only morning I cared to know the time."

"I do believe it is fine!" exclaimed Alice. "Is it William?"

"If you get up, you'll see. It's not pouring cats and

dogs. Get up, Rose. I'll give you ten minutes to dress in. Shall I call Edmund?"

"No," replied Alice Allair. "Mamma forbid it last night She said he was never well throughout the day if aroused up early. And it is true. If you'll shut the door, William, we will soon dress."

Bent upon a congenial expedition, they were not long preparing themselves for it. They were going out to observe the custom of the place on the twenty-ninth of May—that of starting abroad with the sun, to gather and gild oak-balls.

The clock struck six as they went out—William, Alice, and Rose Allair. Quiet enough looked the village in the early morning, but few shutters being open or blinds undrawn. The publicans had been abroad earlier, how-ever; for great branches of oak, nearly as large as trees, were already raised in triumph over their several signs.

"I wonder whether the Vanes are ready, or whether we shall have to wait?" said Alice, as they were ap-proaching a handsome white house, its portico supported by Corinthian pillars. "I hope they will not have turned lie-a-beds!"

"Trust to Harry Vane for that," was William's an-swer. "*He* is never behindhand."

Scarcely were the words spoken, when the door of the house opened, and out leaped an agile, active boy, somewhat younger than William. It was Harry Vane. A dark-eyed, noble, fine boy, careless and random in manner, somewhat too sanguine; but good at heart, truthful, generous. Caroline Vane followed; a hand-some girl. But she descended the steps decorously; not, as her brother did, in a flying leap.

"Halloa! how are you?" shouted out Harry Vane, catching sight of them in the distance.

"Halloa!" came the response from William. "I say! is it not prime to see this splendid morning?" he added, as they came nearer.

"First-rate!" was Harry Vane's answer. "Oh, I said we should have it," he carelessly added. "Some of you croakers prophesied it would be wet. *I* knew better. As if we should get anything but sunshine on the twenty-ninth of May!"

"You always do look on the bright side of things," said William, as they all went on in a heap. The manner of their walking could be called nothing else.

"And you on the dark."

"At any rate, we were justified in croaking, in this instance," returned William. "The rain threatened us yesterday; and had been threatening us for days past."

"The more reason for its changing to fine," argued Harry Vane. "The longest and darkest night gets morning at the end of it. Summer will come in brightly now. You'll see."

"It is to be hoped it will; we have had a pretty good share of all that's dull," remarked William. "The grass wants fine weather. The farmers are complaining."

"Did you ever know the farmers do anything but complain?" returned Harry Vane. "Some of them will be found to find fault with to-day. In fine weather they want it wet; and in wet weather, they grumble that it is not dry. I say, have you met any of the fellows on your road?"

"Not one. Perhaps Robertson's man has turned crusty, and won't let the boarders out!"

"He had better try that on! They'd climb the chimneys, but what they'd come. Or make ropes of the sheets, and get out that way. I would. Robertson would look over it, too; he'd never attempt to stop the oak-balling on this day. Where's Jenniker, I wonder?"

"Talking about Jenniker," said William, "I met him last night. I left my Euripides at school by mistake, and in coming back from getting it, came across Jenniker. He said—— But there's no depending on a word *he* says," broke off William. "He is always romancing."

"Romancing, you call it! He is the greatest—cram teller—in all the school. I use a genteel appellation, young ladies, in deference to your presence," said Harry with a laugh, raising his hat to his sister and to Alice and Rose Allair. "Jenniker will get sent to Coventry one of these days, as sure as he is alive. He will go too far."

"The wonder is, that he has not been sent already. Look at that tale of the traps, the other day! How we were all taken in!"

"What was his romance last night?"

"He said he had just seen Vane—you; and that you were boasting of some jolly news. Then it was decided you were to go to sea."

"That's tolerably correct, for Jenniker. I told him it was nearly decided. It would only have been in keeping had he said I was gone."

"That will never be decided, Harry," interposed Caroline Vane. "Never, in the manner you hope for."

"Won't it, Carry! Do you know what mamma said last night?"

" What did she say?" eagerly asked William.

" I had got into hot water with her; chopped a piece off the dining-room table, in chopping some wood for my new boat. So she told papa I was fit for nothing but the sea, and the sooner I was off the more tranquil the house would be. She was angry at the moment, you know."

" Oh, yes, we all say things at times the very opposite to what we mean," remarked William, rather testily. " Of course she objects in reality just as much as ever?"

" Of course: mothers always do. Mine thinks I shall come to grief among the fishes. Papa laughs at her."

" He sees no objection," observed William, eagerly, who appeared to hold a remarkably strong interest in the point.

" Not he; though he won't say as much to me. The mother thinks—the fishes sparing me—I should return from my first voyage utterly unpresentable; a sort of animal between a Robinson Crusoe and a tattooed wild Indian; and never come into a civilised being again. But, mark you, Allair, she has never said I shall not go."

" What if she did?"

" Don't talk about that," said Harry, hastily. " The having to give up my golden visions would be a climax I'd rather not contemplate. Oh, it won't come to that! Papa sympathizes with me. I know he does. He cared as much for the sea as I do, and they forbid his going. His father was a brave old commander, and fought many a battle under Nelson."

" Who forbid his going?"

" His mother.   She said it was bad enough to have
her husband at sea, without having her son there.
Papa says he never regretted the not going but once,
and that has been ever since.   I suppose I inherit my
taste from him.   The mother often says she is thankful
Frederick has no liking for it."

" And I'm sure I am thankful," interposed Caroline
Vane.   " A grievous calamity, it would be, to have two
brothers, one's only brothers, obstinately bent upon
turning themselves into rough, roving, disagreeable
sailors."

" There are worse misfortunes at sea than that would
be," said Harry, nodding his head.   " However, Carry,
you have your wish as to Fred.   He hates the sea and
all things connected with it.   He would rather do anything on earth than go to sea; turn day-labourer, or
lion-feeder at a wild beast show."

Alice Allair laughed.   "I don't think your brother Frederick betrays great inclination for labour of any sort."

" Not he," said Harry.   " He is the laziest fellow
alive.   It is a good thing for him that he was the eldest
son, born with a silver spoon in his mouth.   Otherwise,
I fear Mr Fred would have stood a chance of starving."

" I can tell you what," said William, " it is the
being born to the silver spoon that does the mischief.
When a fellow knows he has got to work, he does work ;
but if there's not a necessity, he won't make it."

A little bit of wisdom wonderfully true to come from
the lips of a boy of fifteen ; and I daresay you, my
boys, are thinking so.   But you must not give William
Allair credit for it; it was borrowed from his father.
Mr Allair had echoed it in his presence many and many

a time. You will find it to be the case as you go
through life: possibly you have noticed it already.
Fortunes have done more harm than good in this world.
I'd rather see a boy born to honourable work, with a
ready heart to do it, than see him born to a fortune.

"I suppose that's it," returned Harry Vane, in reply to William's remark. "If Fred had not been born
to money, I don't know how he would have lived.
Idleness is his besetting sin! My father says he shall
learn some profession, just to keep his days from being
spent in mischief: Fred says he will not."

"One would suppose the sea, as a profession, would
suit him well, then," remarked William. "A nice idle
life it is, that of a sailor's."

"An idle life!" repeated Harry Vane. "What on
earth are you talking of, Allair? A sailor's work is
never done."

"Rubbish!" cried William. "What can there be
to do on board a ship? Get her once under weigh,
the sails set, and all that, and you have only to walk
about the deck and watch the waves. Except, of
course, in a storm. In calm weather, you may shoot at
the sea-birds all day."

The remark amused Harry Vane excessively. He
stared at William. "Well, you have got a rum notion
of a sailor's life!" he said. "Where did you pick it
up? Just you go out before the mast for a few
months. That would help you to a little general
knowledge in the nautical line."

"I shouldn't mind," was the answer. "Before the
mast, or behind the mast, it would be all one to me, so
that I got there. Anything's better than being chained

to a desk all day; to have to scratch, scratch, scratch, at a pen until your teeth are set on edge, and your eyes are dazzled."

"A desk!" scorned Harry Vane. "I would not stop at a desk, I would not lead such a humdrum life, to be made Lord Chancellor of England. Better cut a fellow's legs off at once!"

"Yes," grumbled William, his tone one of warm resentment. "And they wish to condemn *me* to the life. It's a shame!"

"You have often said you should like the life," said Alice Allair. "You always said so, until you got this sea freak into your head."

"What do girls know about it?" retorted William, who had no better confuting argument at hand; but he laughed good-naturedly at his sister as he said it. "You hold your tongue, Alice."

Alice Allair did not choose to take the hint. "When boys talk of wanting to go to sea," cried she, "it is generally an excuse for a fit of idleness."

"Call it idleness, if you like," said William. "If you had the choice, you might think idleness—which of course means only that you have your time to yourself—preferable to being shut up in an office, glued down to a desk."

"But, for how short a time you would be glued down! At least, closely. Three or four years, and then——"

"Oh, my service to you, Mademoiselle Alice! Years count for nothing, I suppose. What next, pray? I wish I was going for a sailor," continued William, in a gleeful tone, his fair face flushing with pleasure at the thought. "Voyaging about from port to port, and seeing foreign countries! That would be something like a life."

" Oh, it is a jolly life!" burst out Harry Vane, in one of his fits of enthusiasm, to which, it must be owned, he was somewhat given. "The very sight of a ship sends my pulses into a thrill. It does, Caroline; and you need not look at me so mockingly. To see a vessel, with her white sails spread, scudding through the water; to be at the main-top-gallant mast-head and watch her speed, the glorious sea stretched out around; to feel the motion of the good ship as she rides along majestically, the breeze fanning your face, perhaps the sun, a blaze of splendour, rising in the east!—oh, you cannot, any of you, tell the enjoyment that it is. You have never experienced it."

" Ah! that was an unlucky voyage of yours, to Spain and back!" observed Caroline Vane, in a tone of vexation.

Harry laughed out gleefully, and came down from his imaginary perch on the main-top-gallant.

" Why do you call it an unlucky voyage?" asked little Rose Allair. " He did come back."

" I'll explain it," said Harry, before Caroline could speak. "When Captain Marsh was going to Spain with his ship—only a merchantman, you know, of two or three hundred tons—he invited me to make the voyage with him. 'Oh, dear yes, and thank you,' cried mamma. 'He will be dreadfully sea-sick, and that will cure him of his passion for the sea.' Accordingly I started; and was sea-sick, not much, though; and I made the voyage, there and home; and when I got back, poor mamma found she was out in her reckoning. The taste had been confirmed in me. If I had only longed for the sea before, I loved it then. Ever since, mamma and Carry have called it my unlucky voyage."

"It was the most unlucky step you ever took," persisted Caroline.

Harry laughed. "It was a mistake, Carry, that's all," said he, quietly. "As if a trifle of sea-sickness could put me out of conceit of the sea! Why, I'd rather be sea-sick for ever, than not go!"

"Don't talk randomly," rebuked Caroline, who was older than her brother. "Harry, I wonder whether Fred will come out this morning?"

"No, I am sure he will not," replied Harry. "He is above coming out on this morning expedition now. Don't you remember last year?—he said it was his last time. Since Fred passed his eighteenth birthday, he has thought himself a man. Besides, Fred likes his bed too well to leave it, when there's an excuse for stopping in it."

William had fallen into silence. He was thinking how lucky was Harry Vane in possessing a father who saw no ogres in the sea. And thus they reached the Grange meadow, a very favourite resort; and the two boys began to scramble over the stile, as boys will do when in much haste, with little regard to ceremony, or to the young ladies with them.

"There stands Jenniker!" exclaimed William, pointing with his finger.

"And there's another with him! Who is it?"

"Where? Oh, I see, behind the tree."

"Why, I declare it is that ignoramus, Tom Fisher! Of all dolts! Whatever brings Jenniker out with him?"

CHAPTER II.

OF the two boys standing there, one was of a tall, powerful frame, almost a man. That was Jenniker. The other was tall also, but slight and delicate. That was Fisher. In point of fact, Fisher was an overgrown dandy of sixteen, wearing a gold chain across his waistcoat, and two rings on his left little finger; a garnet set round with pearls, and an emerald studded with paste diamonds. His hands were white, his nails faultless, and his coat was cut in the height of fashion. His manner was slow; his brains were not particularly bright. He had been reared in the heart of London, had scarcely ever been beyond it, until this visit, which he was paying to some friends in Whittermead. In his utter ignorance of country sights and country habits, Dr Robertson's pupils, with whom he was brought in contact, felt inclined to convert him into a sort of butt for their mocking sport. What with his dandy-cut coats, his white hands, his rings, his effeminacy altogether, and his real ignorance, the boys enjoyed a treat.

"I say, Vane, what do you think?" called out Jenniker, at the top of his voice, as they approached. " Fisher, here, does not know one tree from another; can't tell an oak from an ash, or a birch from a willow. He says he only knows a poplar; and, that, because it's

tall and thin, like the wooden trees they sell with children's toys in Arcadia."

"I did not say in Arcadia," hastily corrected Fisher,
"I said in the Lowther Arcade."

"Oh, the Lowther Arcade! is it not the same?"
cried Jenniker, putting on the full tide of ridicule.
"My patience and conscience! Not to know a tree
when you see it! I've heard of girls not knowing lots
of things, but I never did hear of a fellow not knowing
trees. You are a curiosity worth taking about the
country in a travelling caravan, Master Fisher."

"Be quiet, Jenniker," said William Allair. "Why
do you begin upon him? He has always lived in London, where there are no trees to be seen."

"Right in the midst of it," put in Harry Vane.
"By Aldgate Pump."

"No, I don't live by Aldgate Pump," resentfully
spoke Fisher. "I have not seen Aldgate Pump above
half-a-dozen times in my life."

"It's by Temple Bar, then."

"Well, Temple Bar is not Aldgate Pump," retorted Fisher. "Aldgate Pump's down Whitechapel
way."

"Are there any trees round Temple Bar, Master
Fisher?" cried Jenniker, returning to the charge.

"You had better go up to London and see," retorted
Fisher, who by no means relished their aggravating
salutation of "Master." "If there are no trees in London, there are plenty outside it. At Clapham, where
my aunt lives, they abound. I daresay I could tell the
names of many, if I wanted to tell them."

"Let's hear, Fisher," said Harry Vane. "Do you

know what these trees are?" pointing to those underneath which they were standing.

Fisher looked up at the trees. He did not know
them, but he did not like to confess to the ignorance.
Another moment, and his face brightened.

"Perhaps they are ivy?" suggested he.

The boys leaned against the trees in their agony of
laughter, and the young ladies—who were not upon
their drawing-room manners—shrieked aloud with it,
driving Fisher wild. Other-young ladies, other schoolboys were running up from various points in the
distance, and the audience promised to be a large one.

"What is there to mock at?" asked Fisher. "Come!
This is ivy that's around them. I know ivy when I
see it, as well as you. My aunt's house at Clapham is
covered with it."

"That's ivy, but the trees are not," jerked out Harry
Vane, in the midst of his convulsion. "We'll give you
three guesses of what the trees are, Fisher; and if you
can't hit upon the right thing, you shall go up them
and get down some boughs."

"Up a tree!" returned the dismayed Fisher, who had
probably never in his experience climbed anything
more formidable than to the top of an omnibus. "I
wish you may get it! My hands and my clothes are
not going to be torn, I can tell you."

At this moment a whole troop of new-comers came
within hearing distance, many of Dr Robertson's scholars
being amongst them.

"Fisher thought these trees were ivys," said Jenniker,
with a very broad grin; Mr Jenniker being rather
addicted to grinning, when he found he could annoy

any friend with it. "We are going to give him three guesses, and if he can't hit upon the right name, he pays forfeit and goes up the tree."

"Why don't you ask me to climb up to the moon at once?" cried Fisher. "You don't get me up the stem of a tree."

"The stem! *the stem!* ha, ha, ha! ho, ho, ho!" shook the boys, holding their sides. "He calls the trunk the stem!"

"The trunk, then," said Fisher. "A thick, round, high trunk like that, where there's nothing to lodge your feet upon! Go up yourselves, if you want somebody to go up. I'd as soon attempt to mount a greasy pole at a fair."

"You'll have to try it," shouted the boys. "Let's hear the first guess. I'll bet the contents of my pockets against Dick Jenniker's, that Fisher does not name them."

"Wouldn't you like it, Harris!" returned Mr Dick Jenniker. "I have got a valuable bank note or two in mine."

Another laugh, at Jenniker's boast of bank notes. Of all the school, his pockets were generally the most empty; he was one who spent his money faster than it came in.

"Come, Fisher, we are waiting for you."

"Oh, well, I don't mind guessing," said Fisher, who was, on the whole, of an accommodating, peaceably inclined nature.

"Let's see. They are not poplars ——"

A shout of derision drowned the conclusion of Fisher's sentence. "Go ahead! That's the first guess."

"That was not a guess at all," disputed Fisher. "I knew they were not poplars."

"That's a fine shuffle!" cried a dozen disputing voices, eager to take any advantage, as boy's voices proverbially are. "You want to do us out of four guesses."

"He knows poplars. Jenniker said so," observed William Allair.

"Yes, yes, let that go," said Harry Vane. "He said he knew poplars, before this was brought up."

"Poplars are tall, straight, upright trees," said simple Tom Fisher. "You can't suppose I mistook these for poplars."

"As tall and as straight as those charming wooden trees that come out of Arcadia. He has been to Arcadia," added Jenniker in an aside explanation to the new-comers, "and knows the trees there. The shepherdesses stand underneath them all day with flowered crooks in their hands. You needn't stare, Mr Fisher. Go on and take your first guess."

"An elm," returned Fisher at a venture, thinking it might be as well not to say anything about Arcadia and the shepherdesses.

"That's one guess. Off again."

"A fir," hesitated Fisher, scanning the tree.

"That's rich, that is! Go at it."

"Well, you give me no time to remember names."

"Plenty of time. Off for the third."

"Is it a mountain-ash, then?" concluded Fisher, who never having, to his knowledge, seen a mountain-ash, thought that might be a reason for this being one.

"All over, all over! He has had his three guesses. Why, you stupid, could you look up at *these* trees, and

B

not know what they are ? Don't you see the balls on them ? Have you never heard of oak-balls ?"

"Haven't I ! We call them oak-apples in London. Is it an oak-tree ?"

"To be sure it is."

"Well, I *was* stupid ! I thought of oak once, and meant to guess it, but you put me out with that bother about the poplars. I said you did not give me time."

"Any donkey would have known it was an oak-tree by the balls, Master Fisher," politely observed Jenniker.

"I saw no balls," grumbled Fisher, who did not relish Jenniker's allusions.

"Don't you see them now ?"

"Yes, now you tell me they are there. But one has to look closely to do it. mixed up, as they are, amongst the leaves."

"Now for the penalty," said Jenniker, who was rubbing his hands as if expecting some choice gratification. "Let us see how a London gentleman can climb."

"I can't climb, I tell you," dissented Fisher. "I won't climb. There !"

"A bargain's a bargain, sir, as we reckon in the country," persisted Jenniker. "A favoured mortal who has been admitted to the sunny plains of Arcady, ought not to be shy of trees. I saw a picture of it once. The ground was moss, and the skies were blue streaked with pink. Come, Mr Fisher."

"A bargain is no bargain when it's made on one side only. That's London fashion. If you think I am going to tear my clothes to rags with your trees, you are mistaken. I mightn't care so much if my tailor were at hand to replenish them."

"You are keeping your friends waiting, Mr Fisher," returned Jenniker with polite suavity. "That's not good manners. Up with you, and fling down a cart-load of sprays. Choose those that have balls. We want to gild them."

"What do you say you want to do?" inquired Fisher, not understanding.

"Gild them. Did you leave your hearing in Arcadia? It is the custom here to carry gilded oak-balls on the twenty-ninth of May."

"How do you gild them?"

"With sheets of gold leaf. Don't you see our paper books here, with the gilt leaves between? The girls gild: perhaps you'll help them. Come, Fisher, no shuffling! Up the stem, as you call it."

"Now, look you here," returned Fisher, taking out a penknife to trim his finger nails. "You won't get me up that tree, if you badger for the whole day; any more than you'll get me up that church steeple yonder. And you may just as well drop the subject as waste your time over it."

There might have been a forced ascent and some disturbance, but the girls—as they had just been un-ceremoniously styled—interfered, saying they would go home if any quarrelling took place. So Fisher was left to repose on mother earth in peace and safety; and the others mounted the trees.

When as many sprays were torn off as were wanted, and the young ladies, many of whom were assembled now, had finished the gilding, they all roved about, enjoying themselves. Conversing, laughing, giving chaff to Tom Fisher and to each other; and plucking the

May and the hedge flowers. Some chased each other over the meadows, snatching handfuls of buttercups and daisies, only to scatter them; plucking, in gleeful merriment, the cowslips and bluebells; seeking for late primroses, for remaining violets. Their happy laughter mingled with the sunshine, with the sweet fragrance of the blossoms; whilst the ringing of the distant bells fell on the ear with the softest melody.

Presently some of them heard the cuckoo, and the rest stood still, their voices hushed. But the bird ceased its notes, and flew away to a distance.

Then the shouting and laughter were renewed, and the running through the long grass on its many coloured flowers, which was not exactly beneficial to the future crop of hay; and it was well, I think, that Squire Jones, to whom the field belonged, had not come oakballing, himself, and caught them there. Little cared they for the hay, that was to be: the present grass and its flowers were enough for them; the cowslips had never been so yellow, the May so pink, the clover so sweet, the bluebells so blue. All things were lovely. The weather had been gloomy so long that this warm sunny morning seemed like a very glimpse of Eden; it might have spoken to them of God.

But these hours of enjoyment passed quickly, and the village chimes told eight all too soon. It was the signal for returning home to breakfast; and away they trooped gradually, bearing their gilded oak-sprays. Other days they had to be in school by seven o'clock, but there was holiday on this one. It came but once a year, that morning ramble, and the gravest schoolboy

among them—to be a freshman probably next year—
was content for the time to be a child again.

As they passed Mr Vane's house, a gentlemanly
young man stood on its threshold, watching the return.
It was Frederick Vane, the handsomest of that handsome family. Had he but been as good as he was
handsome! Harry, only that morning, had called
idleness his brother's besetting sin. As yet, it was
perhaps his worst and only sin: but it is one that leads
to others. A favourite copy is that, given us with our
earliest writing lessons: "Idleness is the root of all
evil."

"Why did you not come with us, Mr Frederick?"
asked one of the passers-by.

He leaned against the stone pillar of the portico as
he answered; leaned in his favourite listless fashion,
and a smile sweet and sunny, but still a listless smile,
parted his lips. Frederick Vane was beginning to
conjugate that noted French verb, the most dangerous
that can make itself at home with a young and attractive man; was repeating over the first person of its
first tense to himself hourly: "*Je m'ennui.*"

"Why did I not go with you?" he repeated. "I
leave the glories of the twenty-ninth of May, getting
up by star-light and oak-balling included, to those who
are still in love with them. I have had my day at it."

"It is not so bad a day yet."

"True—for you. Each age has its favourite kaleide-
scope. Well, Mr William Allair, is that a whole tree
or only some branches of it? You will make your
shoulders ache."

"I'd rather it was a ship's mast," returned William

gaily, but quite without reference to the point, so far
as Frederick Vane or anybody else could see. " Old
Symes the shoemaker was regretting last night that he
could not go out to get a bough for his door, his leg
being worse, so I said I'd bring him one."

" Very polite of you, I'm sure," returned Frederick,
in his thoroughly pleasant, but half mocking manner.
" I hope none of you gentlemen"—throwing his eyes
on the group of boys who had stopped—" will find
yourselves too late for breakfast. It is close upon
nine."

The remark caused a diversion. The being " too
late" for breakfast is not an agreeable prospect to
schoolboys with hungry appetites, and most of them
set off at a canter for their respective homes, or for
that of their head master, Dr Robertson.

William Allair and his sisters did not, at any rate,
find themselves too late for theirs. Mr and Mrs Allair
had waited for them. They had an indulgent home:
one of those not too common, where careful training,
anxious practical lessons, are blended with kindness.
Their young brother Edmund, their poor afflicted
brother Edmund, came forward eagerly as they entered
the house, and he broke into a meaningless shout of
delight as they loaded him with sprays of gilded oak-
balls, and flew on to their plentiful breakfast. It is to
be hoped the rest of the boys found as good a one and
as hearty a welcome.

The meal over, and early attire changed for best,
they waited with feverish impatience for the great
event of the day—the procession, popularly called the
" show ;" a show which had annually enraptured the

younger eyes of Whittermead for not far short of two
centuries.

At half-past ten the church bells rang out for service; not with their Sunday ding-dong—as Dr Robertson's boys irreverently expressed it—but with the same
joyous chimes as in the early morning. Whittermead,
in its loyalty, made a point of attending divine service
on the twenty-ninth of May. And this show, passing
down the street amidst the throng of admiring gazers,
was on its way to attend service as they were.

It was heralded by two great branches of oak, borne
abreast, as large as trees. Large streaming flags and
silken banners followed, preceding a band of music,
which to the ears of those assembled rivalled anything
that could be achieved by the band of her Majesty's
Life Guards. Then came a stream, two and two, of
decorated men, their coats gay with ribbons, and their
hands with a spray of gilded oak. Next appeared a
high spreading canopy of evergreens, garnished with
blossoms and stars, wondrous to behold, underneath
which walked two men, each bearing on his shoulder a
lovely child, fancifully and gaily dressed, half covered
with flowers and ribbons, some with gold and silver
spangles, anything that was beautiful to the eye. They
were called pages. And this was repeated over and over
again—banners, flags, decorated men, green canopies,
and the charming little children; all save the music
and the heralding oak boughs. Now followed the
grand object of interest, especially to the boys—the
Iron Man. He wore a complete suit of iron armour,
hence his appellation, and was mounted on a ponderous
horse. His left hand held the bridle of his charger,

and his right hand grasped a long, sharp spear, which was brandished terrifically, and thrust close to the face of all who ventured within its reach.

"What's that for?" cried Fisher, who had looked on with amazed eyes. "Who is he meant to represent?"

"Oliver Cromwell," said Jenniker.

"No," interposed Gripper, one of Dr Robertson's boys,—in fact, they had most of them collected in a group. "Not Oliver Cromwell. It's meant for Charles himself, I think."

"Then, were I you, I wouldn't 'think' till I could think better," retorted Jenniker to Gripper. "Who ever heard of a king riding in iron armour from top to toe, face and all?—unless he were going to battle. Charles was never called the Iron Man."

"It's meant for Cromwell, just as much as it's meant for Jenniker," observed Gripper to Fisher.

"Jenniker's right," said Harry Vane. "It is meant for Cromwell."

"It is not."

"Very well," said Harry Vane, with a laugh. "Have it your own way, Gripper, and then perhaps you'll live the longer."

"But don't let Master Fisher carry a cock-and-bull story back to Temple Bar with him, informing the natives there that Charles II. rides annually in armour at Whittermead," persisted Jenniker. "He'll be going to Arcadia and spreading it there, if we don't mind."

"Going where?" cried Fisher, who did not catch the word.

"To Arcadia," repeated Jenniker. "So once for

all, Mr Fisher, understand: that Iron Man is old Oliver, if you have ever heard of him."

" What had Oliver Cromwell to do with it ?" asked Fisher.

" Why, don't you know that this is the anniversary of King Charles's restoration ?" said Jenniker.

" Is it ?"

" Well, you are a green goose, Fisher ! Any young lady, but you, would have known that. That's why we go to church."

" What has our going to church to do with King Charles ? He has been dead long enough, hasn't he ?"

" Oh, we go to pray for the continuation of Royalty, and all that. At least, that's the popular understanding."

" And what are those children for ?" again demanded Mr Tom Fisher. " They are not ugly."

" Those are the pages," said Gruff Jones.

" Pages ?" debated Fisher. " I thought they were meant for angels, or Cupids. They look much more like that sort of thing."

" Our nurse used to tell us they were meant for baby angels," timidly observed a young gentleman of eight, who had just been entered at Dr Robertson's.

" Your nurse is an old woman," responded Harry Vane.

" An out-and-out one," added Jenniker. " If they represented angels, they'd dress them with wings, wouldn't they, little muff ?"

" Besides," quoth Gripper, " what had angels to do with King Charles's procession ?"

" Or with Charles, either ?" struck in Monitor Seymour. "If we may believe all that's told, an angel's opposite had more to do with him."

"And Cupid most of all," rejoined Jenniker, with one of his broad grins.

There was a laugh in Jenniker's immediate neighbourhood, and the remark was passed on through the line of senior boys.

"I consider those pages the best worth seeing in all the show," said Fisher.

"Do you hear that?" cried Jenniker to the throng of boys. "Master Fisher considers the pages the best worth seeing! *Is* he a lady, or is he a junior?" Both of which "species"—as Mr Jenniker gallantly expressed it—being known to favour the pages. The schoolboys curled their lips at them, and talked largely of the Iron Man.

Arrived at the church, the procession entered it. The Iron Man, after being assisted from his charger and divested of his spear and helmet, clanking himself up the aisle to his appropriated seat. The boys pressed forward, and got as close to him as they could.

The church was very full; as full as on Sundays: and the service for the restoration of the Royal Family was performed. At its conclusion, a large portion of the congregation hastened, somewhat indecorously, from the church, that they might secure good places to see the show pass back again. It did so in the same order that it had come. The Iron Man, resuming his helmet, contrived, with a great deal of difficulty and some assistance, to remount his steed: but the weighty armour had fatigued him, and the spear was not brandished quite so fiercely as in coming. The pretty dresses of

the pages were tumbled, and their little faces flushed
from their having gone to sleep; but all things looked
as well as before to the general eye: and the ringing
bells again chimed out merrily in the noonday sun-
light.

Ah! what show in after life could ever equal that
rustic show of childhood? Look full at it! boys, girls,
children, look at it! gaze your fill; feast your eyes
upon it ere it shall have passed; another sight and yet
another, before it shall quite fade away in the distance.
Remember it well. It will recur to your memory in
after years as a vision of all that was beautiful. When
you are men and women, it may chance that you will
see sights ten times as fine. The Lord Mayor's show,
with its tinsel and glitter of coaches, and soldiers, and
scarlet robes, and ponderous gold chains; a royal coro-
nation, with its imposing gorgeousness; or a *fête-dieu*
in France—and in that fête there will be canopies and
banners, and lovely children, fancifully habited as are
these pages—and incense-scattering priests in their
golden-worked robes, singing their deep, harmonious
chant; but although their splendour may dazzle the
eye, and a momentary gratification be excited in the
mind, where will be the delight with which you gaze
upon this simple show, now, in your childhood? Gone.
For the fresh feelings that caused you to find rapture
in external things will have left you with your youth.
So, gaze your fill, I say, at the show, and be happy
while you may. Now is the reality of existence; the
conscious, glowing sense of enjoyment in all things:
hereafter little of it will remain to you but its name
and its remembrance.

More pleasure yet: for in Whittermead it was a day consecrated to it. Dinner-parties and tea-parties, and cakes, and sweetmeats, and happy faces; and boys upon their best behaviour, and young ladies radiant in blue ribbons and white muslin, with green and gilded oak-leaves sparkling in their shining hair.

But it came to an end. All things bright must come to an end, as well as all things sad. And the joyous revellers went home to bed in a trance of happiness, to dream it all over again, and to wish that every day in the year was the twenty-ninth of May.

But there was one of those whom you met this morning who did not take part in the feasting or the revelry —and that was Frederick Vane. Frederick Vane departed that day for the great metropolis, where he had been wildly desirous of making a sojourn, and had at length got leave from Mr Vane to do so. It was *his* Arcadia. But one known as yet in imagination only, for he had not been there since he was a child.

CHAPTER III.

My dear boys, I have said that this story is written especially for you. As you go on, you will probably discover why I have written it. I would wish to warn you against disobedience. You have heard of popular fallacies, but I can tell you that there never was a more decided one than that fallacy of yours—the belief that you know better than your parents. How often has a boy come to an issue with his father and mother, and decamped to sea in disobedience! He has picked up that agreeable but most deceptive notion, that the going to sea will prove a remedy for all evils under the sun. Another fallacy.

I make no doubt you must know some who have so gone : I feel sure you know some who are wanting to go. A boy grows dissatisfied, lazy, tired ; tired of all things ; tired of land—or rather of the life he is leading on land—and he thinks he will go to sea. He thinks it will cure him. So it will, with a vengeance. Talk to him of the hardships he will have to encounter ; the endurance he must fortify himself with against the hardships ! You may as well talk to the winds. Did you ever know sons who have gone off to sea in this manner, and have never returned? I have. I have known some who have only gone out to die. It is a common occurrence, this running away to sea: how common. I believe that few of us know or suspect. Some have gone in half opposition; some in downright defiance and disobedience; some, in cunning stealth, running away clandestinely. These boys are often remarkably unfitted for a sea life; and that they find out to their cost. A boy who embraces the sea as a profession ought to have been fitted for it by nature, otherwise it will prove for him the most miserable of all lives that he could lead on earth. Many have sunk under the hardships; many will sink again. Never *you* be tempted to resort to it. Never run away to sea. If any one of you should find the seduction approaching near him, fly from it as you would fly from a pestilence. You can read on now.

At seven o'clock, on the morning following the show of the 29th of May, the boys were all in school, except one. Dr Robertson took a few boarders, but most of his pupils were out-door ones. It was a renowned and expensive school, equal to any in the county. The one not at school was William Allair. He was subject to violent sick headaches, and awoke with one that morning. His absence at these times was readily allowed by Dr Robertson, who knew that while the pain lasted he was incapable of study.

Of all the boys, the two between whom existed the greatest intimacy and friendship, were Harry Vane and William Allair; and yet no two could present to each other a greater contrast. Harry Vane, far in advance of his years, high-spirited, noble, independent, was one of those who are sure to hold sway amongst and rule their fellows. He was universally admired for his daring, yet generous spirit; and his well-known prepossession for, and constant talk of the sea, had created a sort of excited fancy for it in the school. Several had begun to be almost as eager for it as he was. But with this difference; while his liking for it was innate—the prompting of nature—theirs was nothing more than a passing fancy, into which they had worked themselves. Squire Jones's eldest son and William Allair were the most seriously impressed. It was like the hay fever, which had broken out in the school the summer previously. Several got a touch of it, but only one or two were attacked dangerously.

Harry Vane's predilection for the sea was in truth a real one. It had certainly been born with him. Rely upon it, that some peculiar liking, a talent for some certain sphere of usefulness, over and above all others, is born with all of us. Not a boy, amongst you who read this, but has been endowed with qualities by the great Creator that will fit him for some calling in life more especially than for other callings. Try and find out what it is, and then put your whole energy into it.

Before Harry Vane could well speak, he would leap and crow at the sight of his boat. I mean a little toy boat, as large as your hand, which had been given him. Every other toy was thrust aside for this darling plaything. He was six years old when Mr and Mrs Vane went to spend a month or two at the sea-side, and there he saw real boats, real ships, and the sight excited him to intense joy. His nurse reproached him with having "gone mad" after them, and grew sick and tired with her constant visits to the beach and the harbour, for he was ever dragging her there. He contrived, child though he was, to pick up the names applied by sailors

to the different parts of a ship : the jib-boom, the main-
stays, the mizen-mast, the fo'castle, and all the rest ;
and he was for ever using them. His whole talk was
of a ship. Mrs Vane found the names unintelligible,
and told him they sounded vulgar : Mr Vane laughed,
and wondered how the boy picked them up.

One day there arose a sad state of excitement. Harry
was lost. The nurse, with the three children, Frederick,
Caroline, and Harry, had gone to the beach, where she
speedily amused herself gossiping with other nurses,
nurse fashion, while the children, joined by other children, hunted after sea-shells, and dug holes in the sands.
When the time came to collect them for home, Harry had
disappeared. Where was he ? Nobody knew ; nobody
had seen him go away. The nurse was in a dreadful
state of terror : she feared he might have run after the
receding tide, and had got drowned in the sea. The
bevy of nurses ran about wildly ; the children sobbed ;
and some fishermen, who were standing near, asked
the nurse if they should get the drags. To go home
with her tale to Mr and Mrs Vane was the worst task
that servant had been put to throughout her life.

Mr Vane, to whom she spoke first, was not greatly
alarmed. He did not deem it probable that an active
lad like Harry should let himself be drowned in silence ;
and remembering his passion for ships, he thought it
much more likely that he had found his way to the
harbour. Charging the nurse to say nothing to her
mistress, he hastened to the harbour ; and there was the
truant found, having strayed on to a ship. It was a
trading sloop, which had put in the previous night ; and
Harry was asking question after question, as he exa-

mined every corner of it with delighted curiosity, and making himself perfectly at home. The captain was pleased with the little fellow's intelligence and animation. He made much of him; gave him a pretty little model of a ship, so gratified was he at the child's calling the various parts of his own by their nautical appellations; and when Mr Vane got on board, Harry was being regaled with cold plum-duff.

Mr Vane, after some chiding, inquired into particulars. Harry could only plead the attractions of the ships as an excuse for having strolled from the beach. Arrived at the harbour, his attention became absorbed by the sloop; there was something about her build that fascinated him; and he speedily made acquaintance with her sailors. They told him he might come on board at high water, when the ship would be on a level with the sides of the harbour, and he could walk on to her without danger. Harry did not wait for the high water, or for a second invitation, but went on at once, throwing danger to the winds.

" Why, how did you get on ? " inquired Mr Vane, in surprise.

" Down that perpendicular ladder, sir," interposed the captain. " I was on deck, giving some orders, when, what should I see, but a youngster, a babby, as may be said, swing himself on to the gangway and begin to descend ? It made my flesh creep to see him, it did : a little un, like that, walking down such a place : the least false step, and it would have been all over with him, falling from that height. I shouted out to him to get back again, when he turned and looked at me as fearless as you please, which made me shout out louder.

All to no purpose: down he came, as lissome as a cat, and after I'd scolded him for his venturesomeness—which I took French leave to do, sir, just as if he had been a child of my own—we showed him over the ship. And a fine, intelligent youngster he is, as ever I came across. But he seems to have no fear about him."

"He never had any sense of fear," said Mr Vane, in a vexed tone. "He dreads no danger."

"He has been climbing in places aboard this vessel, such as one double his age would look twice at before venturing up," rejoined the captain.

"But you don't look at my ship, papa!" exclaimed Harry, impatiently interrupting the conversation, and exhibiting his present to his father for about the tenth time. "Isn't she a clipper?"

"And what a state you have made your socks and legs in!" resumed Mr Vane. "And look at your nice dress!"

Harry glanced down. He was at the age of pretty dresses and white frilled drawers. The dress was spoilt, covered with dirt and tar.

"Oh, that's nothing," he equably answered, with all the unconcern in the world. "Papa, when I grow up a man, I'll not be captain of such a vessel as this. She's only a sloop. She is neither a brig nor a frigate. But I like her shape."

"He seems to have a hankering after ships," remarked the captain.

"Rather too much of it," said Mr Vane.

At this moment Harry slipped away. The next, he was down the side of the vessel, into a little boat, which had just begun to float with the rising tide. Mr Vane, who could see danger, if Harry could not, ordered him up again; but as soon as he reached deck, he was climbing up the mainmast.

"As handy as if he had served his apprenticeship to it," remarked the captain, following him with his eyes, while Mr Vane called to him to come down. "You'll have to make a sailor of him, sir, it strikes me. He has been going on in the way you see, and talking about ships ever since he has been aboard. When I put that little model in his hand, 'Oh, this is a brig,' says he; and I asked him how he knew it was a brig. 'Why, by the rigging,' quoth he, as 'cute as possible."

"He has certainly a wonderful inclination for the sea," observed Mr Vane. "He seems to take to it naturally, as young ducks take to water. His mother would check it, if she could."

"She'll never check such an inclination as that, sir," said the captain. "When you see it evinced by so young a child, you may make sure it's born with 'em. Older boys put likings on, and get fancies into their heads of their own accord: one of this age don't. I never knew but one have such a hankering after it as this lad seems to have. *His* friends were all against him, but it was of no use."

"He carried the day, I suppose?" remarked Mr Vane, speaking chiefly because the captain was looking at him, and seemed to expect an answer.

"Father, mother, brothers, sisters, grandfathers, and grandmothers, all were against it. They were at him continually; wanting to bind him 'prentice to a trade; inventing all sorts of horrid tales of the sea; foretelling all manner of ill for him, if he went. And that was me."

" You! " exclaimed Harry, who had come down, and was listening.

" Me, myself," repeated the captain. " I loved the sea ; and all their talk was as nothing in my ear. Never, sure, did one love it as I loved it."

" And they would not let you go ? " cried Harry with trembling eagerness.

" Not for a long while."

" And how did you get there at last ? Did you run away ? "

The captain shook his head. " I was sorely tempted to it. They put me to a tailor ; of all trades, the one I mortally hated. Ay, I was sorely tempted, Heaven knows ; and once I had even packed up my traps in a handkercher, what few they were, and had it in my head to start that same night. But somehow I could not do it. Not that I shrank from what was before me, or felt afraid of anything I might have to encounter ; but it came into my mind—listen, my good little boy ! —that God's blessing would never rest upon me, if I left home in rebellious disobedience to my parents."

Harry did not speak. He stood with his earnest, great brown eyes devouring the captain, and the crimson of emotion flushing his clear young cheeks.

" So I stopped. I stopped and tried to like my trade. I tried hard, but it seemed to go against me, and I could make no hand at it. That was the dreariest portion of my life ; I hardly like to look back to it now. After a while things worked round. My father and mother found I was not fitted for an inland life, and at last they consented to my going. Consented freely ; and I departed, happier than a king, and fear-ing not for the future, for they had prayed God to speed me."

"And were you not very glad when you did get right on to the sea?" asked Harry eagerly.

"Very glad; very happy. And God has prospered me from that hour to this, and enabled me to support my parents in their old age."

"And I'll be a sailor, too," cried Harry resolutely. "And if papa and mamma ever want money, I'll send home all mine for them."

The captain nodded his head oracularly. It said to Mr Vane, as plainly as nod could say, that he would never do successful battle with this inclination of his son's. Perhaps Mr Vane did not intend to try.

They quitted the sloop, Mr Vane thanking the captain for his kindness to the boy, and Master Harry was marched home to the tune of a sharp lecture, turning upon young gentlemen who ran away from their nurses, leaving them sick with fright.

This little episode and its attendant circumstances, more especially what he had seen of the lad on board the sloop, strongly impressed the mind of Mr Vane. As the years went on, he began asking himself whether he and Mrs Vane were doing right, to endeavour to thwart by every means in their power this inclination of Harry's for a sea life: he asked himself a more solemn question—whether it had not been implanted in the boy's mind, nay, in his nature, by God.

Mr Vane knew that Harry was—to use a familiar expression—cut out for a sailor. By constitution he was pre-eminently fitted for it, and in that lay a great contrast between him and William Allair. Work was as nothing to him. Of hardships he could bear a vast deal. That which would go far towards killing William Allair, he could endure without a murmur, almost without a thought. For privation he did not care; or, to speak more correctly, what was privation to boys in general, was no privation to him. Were they condemned to bread and water for punishment—while a punishment it would indeed be to the rest of the boys, above all, to William Allair—Harry Vane did not regard it as such. No lad should go to sea without being *sure* of his physical powers, of his strength, of his capability to endure hardships and privation; ay, and to make the best of them.

A famous mechanic, too, was Harry Vane. He could mend anything that came to pieces, put glass in the summer-house window frame, patch up the desks that got broken, and turn out model ships as nicely made as that one given him on board the trading sloop when he was a youngster. A first-rate carpenter was he; and one day he remarked to William Allair that he could rig a jury bowsprit or make a jib-boom for a ship with the best of them in case of necessity.

" What necessity ?" asked William.

" What necessity, now ! Can't you guess ? Suppose we were a thousand miles from land, with no carpenter on board, and our jib-boom went crash in a storm, or a meeting ship carried away our bowsprit ? These are what I should call cases of necessity."

Calm in temper, cool in moments of danger, gifted with great and quick presence of mind, was Harry Vane. But, if he had a sailor's desirable qualities, he had also some of a sailor's faults. Thoughtless, careless, and extravagant was he; swayed by the impulse of the moment, rarely casting a glance to the future. In money matters, none could be more improvident. He never possessed a sixpence. The instant money was given him, it burnt a hole in his pocket, and was scattered right and .left. Off to the shop for sweetmeats, away to the cutler's to leave his tools to be ground, buying up anything exposed for sale that took his eye; spending, in short, to the last farthing, and forgetting to save money to pay for the grinding of his tools. One day he saw three poor shipwrecked sailors, who were asking charity. Of course he had no money; he never had any; and he was a couple of miles from home. Harry was in an agony; he longed to relieve them; if there was one human being his heart yearned to above all others, it was a sailor. He darted into a road-side shop; it was a small shoemaker's; tore off his jacket, borrowed a shilling upon it, gave his name and address, handed the shilling to the sailors, listened to and sympathized with their tale; and went home jacketless.

His daring courage and contempt for danger led him into innumerable scrapes. It almost seemed that he bore a charmed life, so many perilous situations did he come out of unscathed. He made a trouble of nothing. Of a happy and contented mind. the cares and crosses of life—for schoolboys have their crosses and cares as well as other people—passed over him lightly and smoothly as a light fleecy cloud passes over the face of the sun. And here, again, lay a contrast between him and William Allair. The latter would run to meet trouble half way, while Harry would not see it if it came.

Everybody liked Harry Vane : all admired the generous boy and his happy temperament. With rich and poor he was an equal favourite ; and one great characteristic of him was, that he did not understand false pride ; he possessed none of it. One day he would be seen driving along in state in Lord Sayingham's coroneted carriage ; the next he was jolting through the village in the baker's cart. And if, when in the cart, he by chance met the carriage, whilst another boy— could one have been found to allow himself to get into it—would gladly have sunk to the bottom amidst the loaves, Harry sat as erect and unconcerned as before ; the same gay good temper in his eye and smile on his lip, as he lifted his hat to Lady Sayingham. In fact, he possessed that independent, fearless spirit which exalts its owner into a sort of hero, whom all are eager to admire and imitate. Was it any wonder that such a boy should hold sway over his companions ?

But they need not have fallen into the notion that, because Harry Vane was constituted for a sea life, they must be. A few *are* constituted for it. That great Creator who made the sea, has made men fitted to go upon it as their home, their life's work ; but they are but sufficient, units amid the millions ; and where a sailor is *not* fitted for the life and its hardships, it is the very greatest and most bitter mistake to have embraced it. A mistake which brings repéntance in its train, but rarely remedy.

CHAPTER IV.

EMPTY TARTS.

WILLIAM ALLAIR lay in bed with his sick headache. He came down in the latter part of the day. His sisters were out; Mrs Allair and Edmund in the drawing-room. William was taking a chair, when Edmund started up, and, with a vacant smile, drew him towards the sofa.

Poor Edmund Allair! He was an afflicted boy; not being so bright in intellect as he might have been. The neighbourhood called him "silly," and that was not a bad term to express his state. Not an idiot, he had yet little or no power of mind; none of intellect. Trifles amused him, as they might have amused a child of three years old. Could he get a peacock's feather to stick in his cap, he would pace the lawn before the house, glorying in his finery, nodding his head majestically to anybody who would look at him, and bursting out often with his loud, distressing, vacant laugh. There was no hope that his state would ever be ameliorated, or that he would be fit for any occupation. Therefore he would have to be wholly provided for. It was a great affliction to Mr and Mrs Allair, as you may naturally suppose. They were not rich. Mr Allair had also reason to believe that his would be no long life: a disease which carried off his father in his prime,

had begun, he feared, to show its symptoms upon him.
He hoped to last until William should be of an age to
replace him in his profession, so that the practice might
be kept together. William, however, had been allowing certain foolish visions of a sea life to unsettle him.
Very foolish they were as regarded himself; for if ever
a boy was unfitted for hardships and bodily exertion,
that exertion which comprises hard work, it was William
Allair.

He took the sofa offered by Edmund, who sat down
on a footstool at William's feet. Edmund, loving by
nature, held his brother's hand, and frequently kissed
it, gazing tenderly up into his face. William, on his
part, gazed at the sun, then nearing the horizon. He
recalled Harry Vane's raptures the previous morning
over a sea life, and began fancying—well, I hardly know
what he was fancying: something to the effect that *he*
was on the sea, many hundreds of leagues away, all alone
in an open boat. And what with the thought of his
loneliness, which was imaginary; and his intense gaze
at the dazzling sun, which was real, the tears came into
his eyes. He had been cherishing these charming sea
visions all day in bed, by way of soothing his pain. Mrs
Allair, a very pretty, gentle-featured woman, not unlike
William himself, looked up from her book. She was
young yet, and her braided hair had no need of cap,
and the hanging lace of her open sleeves shaded her
rounded arms.

" What are you thinking of, William?"

William roused himself. "Just at that moment,
mamma, I was thinking how beautiful it must be to see
the sun set at sea."

" A sunset is beautiful anywhere."

Another pause. William broke it in a half-caressing, half-sighing tone.

" What a happy life Harry Vane's will be! It is decided that he is to go to sea. Or, as good as decided."

" I make no doubt that, for him, it will be a happy life."

Mrs Allair laid a stress upon the words "for him." William rather fired at that.

" Why for him, mamma? Why not for me?"

" My darling boy, you know why."

" But I must be a sailor. Mamma, dear, *you* might take my part."

" William, we have discussed this subject before," she answered, a shade of annoyance in her tone. " A sailor's life would prove a misery to you. My dear, understand well what I repeat—a *misery*. You are just as unfitted for the calling, as Harry Vane is adapted for it."

" That's what all mothers say," grumbled William. " Harry Vane remarked it only yesterday. One would think the sea was a pool of devouring fire, by the way they seem to dread it for their sons."

" It is not dreaded for all sons. Were Harry Vane my son, I would cordially approve of it for him, and send him away with my blessing."

" And yet you would forbid it to me!"

" I have told you why, times and times. It is out of consideration for your own welfare. You and Harry Vane are differently constituted; and the walk in life that would suit the one, would be especially ill adapted for the other. In bodily powers, in temperament, you

are precisely opposite. Do you remember the cut
fingers, William ?"

William winced.   "As if that were worth bringing
up in argument, mamma ! I was not seven years old."

"But neither was Harry Vane," said Mrs Allair with
a smile. And William was conscious that the argument
was strong against him. The reminiscence was this:—

Once they had been making a boat together. That
is, Harry was the acting man ; William's help chiefly
consisting in sewing the sails : no hand at carpentering
work was he. Master Fisher's hands were not more
delicate than William Allair's.   Sawing, hammering,
cutting, and planing were not in his line : and they
never would be. He was holding a certain piece of
wood steady, for Harry to chop.   Away chopped Harry
with a sharp knife, much too sharp for a young gentleman of seven to possess ; and the knife went a little too
far, and alighted on the fingers of both.   William's was
a mere scratch ; the skin was cut, and a little drop of
blood slowly appeared.   Harry Vane's was cut to the
bone, and the blood came forth in a stream.   William
looked at his own finger, at the little scratch and the
one drop of blood, and was in danger of fainting from
terror ; his lips turned white, his frame trembled.   He
never saw the injury to Harry Vane ; he was too much
absorbed in his own.   Harry Vane carelessly wrapped
his handkerchief round his own wound, led William to
the house, and asked them to attend to him, and then
ran, whistling, off to the chemist, and asked him to "do
it up with a bit of plaster."   The chemist did so ; told
him it was an awkward cut, and that he was a little
hero.   Back went Harry to Mr Allair's, and there he

found—oh, dear!—that poor William had been obliged to be put to bed, sick and faint. So Harry went into the summer-house alone, and continued his work just as though nothing had happened. And this might be taken as a specimen of endurance of each boy. William was of an age now not to care for a solitary drop of blood; but Harry Vane would bear with better firmness the taking off of a leg, than William would the strapping up of a finger, were it cut as badly as Harry's had been. Harry's hands were everlastingly coming to grief: gashes, bruises, abrasions abounded on them. What cared he? He would just tie a handkerchief round till the blood had stopped, and then the places were left, exposed to the dirt and the air, to get well, or not, as they liked.

"William," resumed Mrs Allair, impressively, "a sailor's life, such as some are obliged to lead, would kill you."

"Kill me!" repeated William, in his spirit of disbelief; and perhaps his tone savoured also of mockery. "It is the most charming life going. Look what a fine time they have of it when they go cruising in the Mediterranean!"

"But they can't go cruising in the Mediterranean for ever."

"It must be uncommonly pleasant when they *do*."

"A sailor must bear all weathers and all temperatures," remarked Mrs Vane. "The fierce cold of the poles may stagnate the blood in his veins, and the burning sun of the tropics must glare on him with unmitigated heat. Take up a bar of cold iron in the frozen regions, and it will shrivel the flesh off your hands;

while the dreadful heat, under the line, has sent many to their grave with brain fever. How would you bear these extremes? I have heard you complain bitterly of the cold of a wintry day, and of the heat of a summer one, in mild, temperate England."

"Of course, I should make up my mind to put up with these inconveniences."

"And a very good resolution too, where the inconveniences are inevitable. But, William, they would not by you be less keenly felt."

"Well, if they were, they would hurt nobody but myself. The thought of being planted down to copy mouldy old parchments from morning till night is unbearable. I'd as soon be put in a prison for life."

"Random words, William."

William felt they were; but he had not the grace to say so.

"Never think, my boy, that my opposition to this ideal fancy you have taken up is prompted by any motives, save the urgent wish for your own happiness. Do not interrupt, William; it *is* an ideal, not a real one. Children are inclined to be undutiful and headstrong, thinking that they know best, and preferring to take their own course. They think that the opposition to their own wishes proceeds from a love of rule; but, William, do not you so deceive yourself. Believe me, that nothing on earth can equal the anxiety of a mother for her child."

"Oh, mamma, I know. I know you are anxious for me."

"I wish, my darling boy, that you could be shown the working of a sea life in its true light: that you could witness its toil and hardship, and—in nearly all its cases, when boys have gone as you are wishing to go—its inward pining and repentance. Harry Vane will go to what he loves, for his whole heart is in it; but were you to go, you would find out your mistake too late."

"Gruff Jones is going," returned William, his spirit of disbelief and opposition again rising.

"Gruff Jones!" echoed Mrs Allair. "My dear, you are mistaken. It was only yesterday, when we were looking at the show, that the squire told me the very notion of his being allowed to go was absurd."

"Gruff says he will go, and I think he will," answered William. "He says, if the squire persists in refusing him, he shall run away."

Mrs Allair did not like the words; they seemed to throw some strange chill on her heart. She shook as with a sudden inward fear, and her lips grew white.

"My son, put those dangerous thoughts away from you," she said, in a low, solemn tone, tenderly laying her hand upon his shoulder. "Run away! what sort of a step would that be? Think you, God's blessing would ever rest upon it?"

"Mamma, I was only talking of Gruff."

"It frightens me, William, to hear of a boy running away from home. I never knew good come of such a step yet. I do not think good could come of it. If— What is it, Elizabeth?"

One of the servants had come to call her from the room. William remained, looking at the glories in the western sky, his thoughts far away. A few minutes more, and four or five of the schoolboys came in. On

their way home from evening school, they had resolved
to look up William.

"Here he is!—alive!" began Jenniker. "We
thought you'd be dead by this time, Allair."

"Did you?" returned William, rather crossly. He
could not put up with "chaff" as well as some of the
boys could. Of a gentle, timid, yielding disposition,
he was less fitted for the rough life of a public school
than some of them were. His very appearance was
indicative of his sensitive nature, with his refined features, his soft blue eyes, his bright complexion, and his
fair, wavy hair.

Gruff Jones, one of the visitors, flung himself into a
chair with an action of impatience. He was a short,
stout lad, the eldest son of Squire Jones, a gentleman
of some importance at Whittermead. The boys had
nicknamed him "Gruff" on account of some peculi-
arity in his voice.

"It is of no use talking to the governor," Gruff
began, in a grumbling tone. "He won't as much
as hear me name the sea now. He'll never let me
go."

"Bother him till he does," advised Jenniker.

Gruff shook his head. "He won't be bothered. If
I begin but with half a word, he shuts my mouth up.
I *will* go!" added the young gentleman, stamping his
foot. "The thing is, if he sets his face dead against
it, how am I to get there?"

"Run away," said Jenniker.

"Jenniker told me yesterday you had made up your
mind to run away," interrupted William Allair.

"Well, I don't know," mused Gruff, who was rather

a mild sort of boy, in spite of his gruff voice. " I'm
afraid it wouldn't do."

"Not do!" echoed daring Jenniker. " Just hear
him!" he added, turning to the rest. " He's afraid it
wouldn't do to run away! If you want to do a thing,
and other folks say you shan't, the best way is, to cut
the matter short by doing it."

Gruff considered. Apparently he did not see his
way clear. " I might not get safe off," debated he.
" The squire might catch me up and bring me back,
and have me before him on the bench, as a vagabond.
You don't know what he is when he's put up. He'd
no more care for putting one of us in prison, than he
cares for committing the poachers. Besides, where
could I run to? I should have neither money nor
outfit; and there'd be no fun in going to sea without
your uniform."

" Have it your own way," said Jenniker. " If you
won't bother the squire into sending you, and won't
start on your own account, you must humdrum on at
Whittermead for life, feeding your own innocent sheep,
and cultivating your crops of mild turnips. They'll
put you on the bench, perhaps, when you are of age,
and you can sit there and commit poachers on your
own account."

Gruff Jones did not like the bantering tone. " What
would you advise me to do, Jenniker?" he asked.

" You needn't come to me for advice. I wash my hands
of milksops," he added, making a motion of rubbing one
hand over the other. Gruff looked irresolute.

" Shall you run away, Vane, if they don't let you
go?" he asked.

"No," said Harry Vane. "I expect they will let me go."

"But if they don't, I said?" persisted Gruff.

"Then I must put up with it as I best can. I should never run away. No good comes of that."

"Better run away than be kept from doing what you like," spoke up Jenniker.

"Better *not*. An old merchant captain told me once that running away never prospered anybody. I don't believe it does. *I* am not going to run. Stuff!"

"I don't know but what I shall have to run," struck in Jenniker. "I'd not bet upon it."

"It won't matter so much for you," responded Harry Vane. "You have no father to disobey."

"No. And the commandments don't tell us we must honour our uncles and our step-aunts," returned the incorrigible Jenniker. "I am getting into hot water at home."

"Worse hot water than usual?"

"A sight worse. But I have paid them out. There's a party gone to Cummerton Castle to-day—a picnic."

Jenniker's face was so radiant with mischief, his tone so suggestive, that the boys inquired what his joke was.

"I was invited to this picnic, mind you; I know I was, for Mildred whispered it to me some days ago," he answered. "I thought I was going, until last night. No, if you please! My uncle and step-aunt gravely told me I should only be in mischief if I went, and spoil the party. I have served them out."

"Don't say *step*-aunt, Jenniker. It does sound so!"

"I *shall* say it. She's no aunt of mine, and I shan't call her one. Well, it made me mad, as you may

guess, finding I was to be put out of the fun, so I
thought I'd spoil theirs a bit. The folks were to take
their own provisions. One lot took meat; another lot
took poultry; another, cheese and bread-and-butter;
another, wine; another, knives and forks, and dishes
and spoons, and tea-kettles and glasses, and all that
sort of rattletraps. It fell to our lot at home to find
pastry and custards. All yesterday afternoon, as soon
as the show was over, my step-aunt, and Mildred, and
the cook were melting themselves over the kitchen fire,
boiling the custards, and baking the tarts. Mrs Jenniker did not make big pies; about a couple of hundred
of little tarts; just what we could take in at a mouth-
ful, you know. I heard her say to Mildred they'd be
more convenient to carry than pies in dishes. All
covered they were; no jam to be seen: perhaps she
thought it would run out on the road——"

"My! shouldn't I like to have been before that col-
lation!" struck in Gruff Jones, while the whole of the
boys stood with watering mouths.

"Don't interrupt," said Jenniker, winking his eyes.
"'Twas all got ready by night: custards corked up in
wide-mouthed bottles, and put in a hamper; tarts
packed in another hamper. And then it was I found
I was not to get any, or any fun, either. So down to
the cellar I crept, when the house was in bed, and got
at the dainties."

"Did you finish the lot, Jenniker?" asked the boys,
in a despairing state of envy that the luck had not
been theirs.

"I didn't eat them; I spoiled them," said Jenniker,
winking again—a very ugly accomplishment, but Jen-

niker had some ugly ones. " I uncorked the custard
bottles, and poured in a little shalot vinegar ; and you
may guess what the flavour was then, besides turning
the stuff to curd. Then I took the tops off the tarts,
all neat and clean, with my penknife, and devoured
the contents, and fastened on the tops again with white
of egg ; leaving them just the same, to look at, as they
were before."

"Jove! what a treat! Was it all jam?"

"Jam, and other stuff. Apple, and lemon, and
rhubarb, and green goosegogs—oh, about fifty sorts,"
answered Jenniker. " I demolished it all. I was down
there three hours, stuffing, and accomplishing the job
neatly. When I came up, nobody could have told that
so much as a finger had been laid upon the hampers.
Hadn't I the stomach-ache, though, towards the morning! They'll be returning home, that picnic lot, in
about an hour's time."

The boys sat in a trance of delight, devouring the
tale as eagerly as Mr Jenniker had devoured the insides of the tarts. And poor Edmund Allair laughed
and crowed incessantly, without understanding what
there was to laugh at.

CHAPTER V.

ONE black sheep will spoil a flock. One black boy—speaking with regard to the sheep and the boy meta-phorically—will spoil a whole school.

Harry Vane infected his companions with a love for the sea; but he was not the black sheep. That boy was Jenniker, the eldest of them all.

Nothing overwhelmingly bad, either, was there in Jenniker. He possessed no very evil habits; he did not thieve or kill. But Jenniker was daringly self-willed: somewhat loose in principle; inclined to dis-obedience and rebellion; and Jenniker's shortcomings in these respects worked contagion in the school.

In some respects poor Jenniker was to be pitied. He had not the advantage, the safeguard, of a happy home. Left an orphan at an early age, he had been brought up by an uncle and aunt. His aunt was fond of him and treated him well; his uncle also treated him well during her life. But she died; and the time came when his uncle took another wife, and the second Mrs Jenniker set her face against the boy. There had been war to the knife ever since. And it is not improbable that Jenniker would have made short work of it and run away long ago, but for the earnest pleadings of his sweet cousin Mildred.

He went home, after boasting of his exploits, as to

the tarts, at Allair's. Mr Jenniker, a wealthy farmer, lived about a mile out of Whittermead, at the Manor Farm. Jenniker—Dick, he was generally called at home—was deep in the preparation of his lessons for the following morning, when the carriage drove up, containing his uncle, Mrs Jenniker, and Mildred. Some friends were with them; they had come to spend the evening; and Jenniker escaped anger for the time. Mildred came to him in the study, gave him an account of the day's proceedings, told him the trick was assumed to be his, and that Mrs Jenniker vowed vengeance against him.

Jenniker only laughed. But when the guests had left, the storm fell upon his head, Mr and Mrs Jenniker heaping reproaches upon it. Jenniker retorted, and there was an angry scene. The boy—he was not much more than a boy, though he was so big and tall —spoke out as he had never spoken. Mildred burst into tears. These disputes made the sorrow of her life.

"Such a row!" said careless Jenniker to the boys of his desk the next morning at early school. "They quarrelled with me, and I quarrelled with them."

"But about the tarts, Jenniker?" cried the boys, eagerly. "How did they find the trick out?"

"I'd give a guinea to have been there and seen the fun!" responded Jenniker. "When the time came for the repast to be spread, the company turned out their hampers, and my step-aunt turned out hers. The tarts looked all right, but the custard didn't. 'My dear,' says uncle to her, 'your custard has turned.' 'My custard turned!' says she: 'it's not likely;' for if there's one thing she prides herself upon, it's the making of her cheesecakes and custards. So my uncle tastes the custard, and finds it sour—all turned. 'It's my belief there's vinegar in it,' cried he. So that put her up. 'What should bring vinegar in my custards?' she asked. 'Taste it,' returned uncle. Well, she did taste, and the company all round tasted, and they found a flavour of onions in addition to the vinegar, and————"

"Stop a bit, Jenniker! How did you get at this?"

"Mildred told me. I wish you wouldn't put a fellow out," responded Jenniker. And he hastened to continue his story, adding to it, no doubt, sundry flourishings and embellishments of his own. "The custard was thrown away, and the dinner proceeded. When the meats were done with, the tarts came on. You know old Mother Graham? Well, she was served first, being the oldest and fattest. 'What sort will you take, ma'am?' asks Mrs Jenniker, who presided over her own tarts. 'I'll take a gooseberry, ma'am,' replies Mother Graham. So Mrs Jenniker looks at her private marks, and sent her a gooseberry, and Mother Graham takes a good bite at it. 'Goodness me, ma'am!' she shrieks out, 'you have forgotten the fruit!' 'Forgotten the fruit!' repeats Mrs Jenniker, resenting the rudeness. 'Don't, mother!' whispers her son, the parson, to her —for *he* thought it was nothing but rudeness—'Mrs Jenniker always puts plenty of fruit in her tarts.' 'But there's none!' cries out Mother Graham to him; and she pulls the tart apart before the company. This flustered Mrs Jenniker; she told Mildred angrily that it was her carelessness, for it was she who had filled the tarts: and she hands Mother Graham another. 'But what tarts *are* these?' cries Mother Graham, taking a

bite as before. 'They have got no insides to them.'
Mrs Jenniker, in a fearful passion, cut a few open, and
found they *had* no insides, but were hollow and empty.
Mildred says I should have seen the consternation.'

The desk was in an ecstasy. It had not been treated
to such a tale for many a day.

"They laid the blame upon my shoulders at once,
my uncle and step-aunt," went on Jenniker, "vowing
vengeance upon me. They said I had done it on purpose to vex Mrs Jenniker, and they told the company
so. They told the company I was vile and undutiful,
the wickedest fellow of a nephew going; and ———"

"How did they know it was you who did it?" interrupted one at the desk.

"Oh, they guessed that. Of course, they would
guess it. I knew they would when I was demolishing
the tarts. Mildred would not do such a thing, and the
servants wouldn't; so there was nobody to pitch upon
but me. If———"

"Silence!" interrupted the voice of Dr Robertson.

The room was a large one. Dr Robertson's desk was
placed in the middle; the desk at which sat these boys
was at the upper end, extending alongside the wall.
At the other end of the room, opposite to their desk,
was the entrance door. Jenniker waited until the echo
of the master's voice had died away, and then began
again.

"You should have heard the uproar there was last
night. They abused me, and I abused them. I told
that step-aunt of mine a bit of truth, and she didn't
relish it: that the Manor Farm had been a pleasant
place until she stepped into it, but it never would be

again. *That* angered my uncle, and he promised to get me punished to-day by Dr Robertson. He had better!"

Vain defiance of Jenniker's! Scarcely had it passed his lips, when the schoolroom door opened, and some one entered it. The boys, who had been so eagerly enjoying the tale, recoiled with surprise.

"Jenniker! look there!"

Jenniker did look. It was his uncle, Mr Jenniker. He did not appear angry, but there was an expression of cold firmness on his face that spoke volumes to Jenniker, who knew all its turns. That Mr Jenniker was in earnest respecting the threatened punishment, his coming thus early before breakfast proved. He went aside with Dr Robertson, and spoke with him for some minutes in a low tone.

What he said was never known. It was rumoured in the school afterwards that he put the affair in a very strong light indeed, and accused his nephew of *theft*. At any rate, whatever may have been the precise nature of the representation, he succeeded in his demand for extreme punishment. The doctor called Jenniker up, spoke a few severe words, summoned his man-servant, and ordered Jenniker to prepare for a flogging.

Jenniker's face flushed. With all his escapades, he had never been flogged; indeed, it was a punishment scarcely ever resorted to by Dr Robertson. "What have I done to deserve a flogging?" asked he.

"Your own conscience can tell you that," replied the doctor. "Mr Jenniker has satisfied me upon the point."

"I only played them a lark, sir," said Jenniker, looking from his uncle to the doctor. "I took the insides out of some tarts for their picnic yesterday. That does not merit a flogging."

"Your conduct in many ways is incorrigibly bad, I find; it has been for some time," returned the doctor, taking out his great birch. "I hope this punishment will have an effect upon you."

"What have you been telling him, uncle?" angrily asked Jenniker.

"The truth," curtly replied Mr Jenniker.

"Hoist him," said Dr Robertson to his servant, giving the word of command in a sharp tone, while Mr Jenniker stood with an impassive face, never speaking, watching for the infliction of the punishment.

"I won't be flogged! I won't!" said Jenniker, loudly and rebelliously. "I have done nothing to deserve it."

Resistance to power in a case like this, where the might lies all on one side, is of little use, and Jenniker found it so. He was seized upon, his back bared, and the birch soundly applied.

It was not a pleasant sight: he was too big to be flogged; and it looked more like punishing a soldier than a schoolboy. Jenniker was the tallest in the school, standing over five feet eight.

"I hope you'll remember this," cried Mr Jenniker to him, with his disagreeably calm impassiveness, when the punishment was over. And, taking leave of the doctor, he quitted the school.

Jenniker returned to his desk, sullen and resentful. There was a look on his face that boded no good, could the boys have read it.

"How did it taste, Jenniker?" came the intruding whisper.

There will always be found some boys ready to pay off these shafts. Jenniker heard it, and brought down his fist on the desk with a fierce word.

"The first of you that throws that flogging in my teeth, or even gives me so much as a look over it, shall be licked into powder. I promise it. Now! Go on, if you dare: you are none of you strong enough to fight with me."

In a trial of strength, Jenniker was a match for almost any two boys in the school; and, as none had a wish to be converted into "powder," they decided to let Jenniker alone. It was their wisest plan. Of a good-humoured, careless nature in general, Jenniker, when aroused—though it took a good deal to do it—would show out (as the school expressed it) as savage as any wild heathen.

So the desk was silent, and by and by the morning school broke up for breakfast. Jenniker was the first to depart. He strode across the long room with steps so fierce and swift, that the boys could only watch him in something like surprise. When they got out, he had disappeared.

The school collected in a knot, talking over the great event of the morning. A few who bore ill will to Jenniker declared that it "served him right," but the popular opinion of the majority was that it was "too bad." If Jenniker was insolent—and they all knew he could be that, when it pleased him—that step-aunt, of his, was cruel: always "on at him," "thwarting and aggravating him continually." If stern old Jenniker——

The conclave was interrupted by Dr Robertson, apparently by accident. He halted, and told the boys

they had better hasten home to breakfast, if they had a
mind to be in time for ten o'clock school. And the
boys had no resource but to disperse.

When they reassembled after breakfast, Jenniker was
not one of them. His place remained empty. The
boys did not wonder much : it was just what was to be
expected from independent Jenniker. And even bets
were laid one with another whether he would make his
appearance after dinner.

He did not—as the event proved. The place at his
desk was still vacant in the afternoon. Dr Robertson
said nothing; but he was probably resolving upon a
further punishment for the gentleman, for this daring
attempt at insubordination.

Not a sight did the boys catch of him all day, in
school or out. They were in the habit of assembling at
Dr Robertson's in the evening, to prepare their exercises and lessons for the ensuing day. It was not a
compulsory attendance this, and no masters were present; one of the under ones occasionally would be there,
but it was not very usual. It was thought Jenniker
would probably come, and the school mustered in force;
but they were disappointed. There was no Jenniker.

" He won't show himself until to-morrow morning,"
cried Gripper. " I said from the first he'd not come
again to-day."

" And right of him too," said Gruff Jones, who had a
hasty tongue. " I'd not, I know, if I had been flogged
as Jenniker was."

" Suppose we go up to his place, and see him ?"

" Suppose you do nothing of the sort!" retorted
Monitor Seymour, with decision. " Jenniker won't

thank any of you fellows for intruding on him. Let him have his smart out; it will be over with to-day."

And for once the boys thought well to follow advice. It might be as well to let Jenniker's temper cool down.

CHAPTER VI.

THE following day was Friday. The boys flew to early morning school with unwonted alacrity, getting there before seven. They cherished a nameless curiosity to see how Jenniker looked after his flogging.

Jenniker, however, chose to be late. Dr Robertson also was late, it being nearly eight when he entered the room. Casting his eyes around as he took his seat, he noted the absence of Jenniker.

" Where's Jenniker ? " he called out.

" He is not come, sir."

" Not come ! " repeated Dr Robertson. " Where is he then ? " he added, after a pause.

There was no reply.

" Have any of you seen him ? " asked the doctor.

The whole school spoke now. None of them had seen him. They had not seen him since he left the school the previous morning, after the flogging.

Dr Robertson ran his eyes over the boys, and called up Vane.

" Go to the Manor Farm," he said. " Inquire why Jenniker is not at school, and say I demand his immediate attendance. Don't linger on your errand, Vane," sharply added the doctor, as a particular injunction to his messenger.

Harry Vane liked the expedition excessively. The school envied him, and resentfully thought Vane was always in luck. A scamper up to the Manor Farm was rather more agreeable, on a sunshiny June morning, than the bending over the school desks at their horrid books, as they termed them; and the "horrid books" did not get much of their attention during his absence.

Harry Vane was shown into the breakfast room at the Manor Farm. Pretty Mildred was alone in it. Her papa had gone riding round his farm, and Mrs Jenniker was not down. "I have come to ask about Jenniker," said Harry. "Robertson is in such a temper."

Mildred looked alarmed. "What about him?" she asked. "Is he ill?"

"Is who ill?" returned Harry Vane, not understanding.

"Richard."

"Richard!" repeated Harry. "I don't know what you mean, Mildred. He has not been near school since yesterday morning. I have come to order him there."

Mildred's face began to grow white. The words brought to her she knew not what of dread. "He has not been home since yesterday morning," she whispered. "Where is he? What can have become of him?"

Harry Vane could only look at her in surprise. Where *could* Jenniker have gone?

"Was it a dreadful flogging?" asked Mildred, in a shuddering whisper.

"Pretty smart," was the answer. "What did he say about it?"

"I have not seen him," replied Mildred. "He has not come home. When papa came into breakfast yesterday morning, he told my aunt that he had been having Dick punished. It made me feel sick when he

spoke of the flogging, and I burst into tears.   Papa was
angry : he said I was always ready to take Richard's
part ; and when I wished to ask further about it, he
would not answer."

"But what an odd thing that he should not have
come home !" ejaculated Harry Vane, unable to overcome his surprise.

"*I* wondered," said Mildred, doing her best to choke
down her fright and her tears.   "Papa said, no doubt
Dr Robertson had kept him for further punishment."

"What a notion !" returned Harry Vane.   "When
a flogging's over, the punishment's over."

Mildred was shivering.   "When night came on, and
still Richard did not come, what I thought was, that
papa had requested Dr Robertson to keep him.   Papa
did not seem in the least uneasy, and Mrs Jenniker
never mentioned Richard's name throughout the day."

"Where can he have got to, though ?" reiterated
Harry.   "If I go back without him, Robertson will be
in a rage."

"He is not here," was all poor Mildred could reply.
"Oh, I wish they had not flogged him !   What will be
the result of it ?"

It was hastily decided between them that a servant
should accompany Harry Vane back, partly, as Mildred
hoped, to gather some news of Richard ; partly, as
Harry suggested, to bear out the information that
Jenniker was *not* at home.   Mildred called the man,
gave him his orders, and they departed.

Harry Vane looked flushed when he entered the
school.   Mr Jenniker's servant awkwardly touched his
hat, and then stood with it in his hand near the door.

"If you please, sir, Jenniker is not at home," said Harry, addressing Dr Robertson. "He has not been home since yesterday morning."

"Then where is he?" uttered the amazed doctor, after a pause, given to digest the news. "Did you see Mr Jenniker?"

"No, sir, he was out on the farm. I saw Miss Mildred. She said her papa, when he found Jenniker did not go home, thought you had kept him for punishment."

"I should not be likely to keep him all night, had I detained him for the day. Mr Jenniker might have known that. What do you want, my man?" the doctor added, turning to the servant.

"Miss Mildred gave me orders to come here, sir, and ask what you thought—as to where Master Richard can have got to," was the man's reply. "She seems quite alarmed, sir."

"I cannot tell at all," said the doctor. "I can form no opinion upon the subject, tell Miss Jenniker, unless it is that he is hiding somewhere. It is very bad conduct. Mr Jenniker ought to be informed immediately."

The man, giving his hair a touch to the doctor, and another general touch to the school, quitted the room.

Dr Robertson looked round on the throng of boys. They were partaking of the excitement, as to Jenniker. Not one had his eyes on his duties.

"Are you sure that none of you have seen Jenniker since yesterday morning?" he asked.

The boys replied that they were. Quite sure.

"Did he say anything when school was over? Or give any clue as to where he was going?"

E.

A boy named Wilkins answered. He fancied the doctor looked at him particularly.

"Jenniker did not wait to say anything, sir. He went out of school first, the moment the doors were opened. I don't think he spoke a word to any of us after the flogging, except to warn us that he would bear no comments upon it."

"It is very strange where —— " Dr Robertson's words were arrested by the reappearance of Mr Jenniker's servant. The man came in, looking wild, his face excited, his hair standing on end.

"He has gone and enlisted for a soldier!" gasped he, altogether ignoring ceremony.

"What? Who?" exclaimed the doctor, while the whole school, including the under masters, stood up in commotion.

"Master Richard has, sir. As I went out from here, Bailiff Thompson was a passing, and he stopped me. He says he see our Master Richard in Burchester last night, along with a recruiting troop, and he had got colours a flying from his hat. He has gone and 'listed, for certain," added the man, quite in an agony.

Dr Robertson paused; he did not much like the news. "Make the best of your way home to your master, and acquaint him," he presently said. "Is Thompson sure that it was young Jenniker?" he resumed, almost unable to take in the unpleasant tidings.

"There can't be no mistake, sir. Thompson says he spoke to him. I always said as it would end in something bad," concluded the man, as he turned to depart. "Master Richard was so random and self-willed: he never cared for nobody. Master and mistress have crossed him, too, a good deal of late."

The tidings were giving Dr Robertson very great concern. When the school broke up for breakfast, he proceeded to the Manor Farm. Mr Jenniker had returned home then, and was in possession of the news.

"He must be seen after," said Dr Robertson.

"Not by me."

"Seen after, and bought off," continued the doctor.

"Not by me, I say," repeated Mr Jenniker. "He is a wicked, ungrateful boy. A little taste of the world's hardships will do him good."

"But there's no knowing what trouble and mischief he may get into," urged the doctor. "There's no foreseeing where it may end."

"It is his own look out," replied Mr Jenniker. "As he has made his bed, so shall he lie upon it."

And nothing was done for Richard Jenniker. Had Mr Jenniker possessed boys of his own, he had possibly been more lenient to his nephew's faults. He was what is called a gentleman farmer, had plenty of money, and intended Richard to be a farmer after him. This, Richard had stoutly repudiated. He had "no liking that way," he urged, and wished for a more stirring life. Jenniker possessed a trifling patrimony; not much. He was inclined to be wild, and was thoroughly idle. "A scamp of a boy," Mr Jenniker had been in the habit of calling him; and he called it him more forcibly now. There had been frequent disputes between them, it turned out, touching Richard's future occupation: he was to have left school at the midsummer, now close upon them.

There was no doubt that Richard Jenniker had felt
the disgrace of the flogging keenly. It appeared that
instead of going home to breakfast afterwards, he proceeded on foot to Burchester, a large city, some seven
miles distant. Not, probably, with any ulterior aim:
anywhere, anywhere out of Whittermead; anywhere
to walk off his angry feelings, his bitter humiliation.
Richard Jenniker was in that frame of mind when it
seems a relief to run away from oneself; but that, as
we are all aware, can never be done. He scarcely
cared what became of himself; he was at enmity that
day with the whole world: even the thoughtless taunt
of one of the boys at his desk, "How did it taste, Jenniker?" bore its own sharp sting of pain. He was
at enmity with Whittermead: he'd never go back to it,
he vowed to himself in his rage. He would have gone
back to it, there's no doubt, that night or the following
day, according to the time his anger took to cool, had
not circumstances ordained it otherwise.

Miserable, unhappy, ill-fated circumstances! No
sooner had he entered Burchester, than he fell in with
a recruiting sergeant. The man accosted him with his
wiles, and Jenniker, yielding to the fit of recklessness
upon him, enlisted. The process over, some flying
streamers were affixed to his hat; and he with the rest
of the raw recruits, their streamers flying also, took a
march through the town under convoy of the watchful
sergeant, and were met, as you have heard, by Bailiff
Thompson, who brought home the news.

Whittermead was divided in its opinion. Some laying the blame wholly on Richard Jenniker; others
deeming that Mr and Mrs Jenniker deserved at least a

share of it. Had less harshness and some kind persuasion been extended to him, they argued, Dick would have turned out better. But conflicting opinions amounted to nothing: what was done, was done.

Mr Jenniker would not buy him off. The most persistent of all his urgers, that he should do so, was Dr Robertson, who may have had a certain flogging pricking his conscience. Mr Jenniker totally refused, and at length declined to listen. " Dick had enlisted of his own accord, and Dick should abide by it," was all he said. So poor Dick was left to his fate.

Short work is sometimes made of it, I would have you to know, young gentlemen, when a boy takes the extreme step that Jenniker had just taken. On the very morning that his loss was discovered, at the very hour that Harry Vane was relating to the doctor the fact of his not having gone home, Jenniker was in the guard's box of a railway train, speeding to Portsmouth. The rest of the simple recruits were with him, all that the crafty sergeant, by any plausibility of wile and persuasion, had been able to enlist. The regiment to which they had sold themselves was collected at Portsmouth, under orders to embark for India. This news travelled to Whittermead and to the Manor Farm.

Others had done urging Mr Jenniker on the subject of his nephew: they had found it a hopeless task. Mildred pleaded still.

" Papa! papa! " she uttered, in much agitation, and the tears streamed down her gentle face; " *pray* buy Richard off! Do not let him go out in this way! He may never return. Buy him off! oh, buy him off! "

" It is no business of yours, Mildred, that you need

concern yourself," was the reply of Mr Jenniker, reso-
lute in his obduracy.

"Think of his hard life!" she wailed.

"I make no doubt it will be hard," equably returned
Mr Jenniker. "He should have thought of its hardships himself, before entering upon it. What people
sow, that must they reap."

Never was there a truer axiom. Take note of it,
boys. Accordingly as you sow, so you will reap. Put
good seed into the ground, and good fruit will come up,
and bring a blessing with it. But, if you scatter the
bad seed broadcast, it can but return upon you its own
recompense. Kind brings forth kind.

CHAPTER VII.

JENNIKER's escapade made great noise in the school. It left its impression behind it: and that gentleman was some way on his voyage to India with his regiment, before another syllable was heard from any one boy about "running away." But the impressions stamped on the minds of schoolboys are effaceable as prints on the sea-side sand; and as the time wore on, old feelings began to resume their tendency. The next to rebel was Mr Gruff Jones.

Not to run away. Mr Gruff possessed too much innate conscientiousness to attempt that; and he was besides of a timid temperament. But he did what Jenniker had once advised him to do: he worried his father.

"Let me go to sea! I can't stop on land. I shall never be happy unless I go to sea." And this was the burden of his song night and day. Squire Jones grew weary. What was more, he grew provoked and angry. Constant dropping will wear away a stone; and young Mr Gruff's everlasting refrain wore away the patience of Squire Jones.

"Very well, young gentleman," said the squire, one evening when Gruff was pitching it rather strongly. "We'll have an end to this. I know of a trading vessel that's going to the Mauritius, three hundred and thirty tons burthen, and I'll bind you apprentice to the captain."

Gruff was in an ecstasy. Little cared he, in his blind wilfulness, how he got to sea, provided he did get there. Apprentice or not apprentice; a trading lugger or a fine frigate; before the mast, or a gentleman middy; it all seemed one to Gruff. His experience had to come.

"Is it true, papa?" gasped Gruff, in an agony of dread lest the squire was only joking. "Will you really let me go?"

"Don't I tell you so?" returned Squire Jones. "The opportunity is offered me of placing an apprentice on board that ship, and I'll place you. As you will go, you shall go."

Gruff, scarcely knowing whether he stood on his head or his heels, tore off to find his friends, the boys of his own desk. They were at their evening work in the school, and Gruff astonished them by bursting into the room like a lunatic, and flinging his cap into the air.

"I am going at last!" he cried, when he could speak for want of breath and excitement. "The squire has come to his senses."

"Going where?" they asked. "To sea?"

Gruff nodded, nodded fifty times; Gruff made pirouettes over the desks; Gruff executed a wild dance round the room on his legs and head. The school came to the conclusion, that if Squire Jones had come to his senses, his son had undoubtedly lost his. That day two months the unhappy Gruff would have performed unheard-of penance to be on land again; *for he had then found out what a sea life was,* to his miserable cost. But that is neither here nor there. At present, seeing it only in prospective, it was all *couleur de rose* to Gruff.

"I say, Gruff, tell us how you are going. In the navy?"

"Navy be hanged! I am too old. How can I go in that when I have never been entered? The squire knows of a trading vessel bound for the Mauritius, and he says he will put me apprentice to the captain."

One of the boys gave a shrill whistle. It was Gripper, who was *not* infected with the sea mania. Gripper knew somewhat more of ships, and the work of those who had to man them, than most of the boys did. "Is she a big vessel, Gruff?" asked he.

"Three hundred and thirty tons."

Gripper turned up his nose. "Oh! a dirty little trading sloop! I'll tell you what, Gruff: if the squire's not doing this to give you a sickener, call me a Dutchman."

"You are an idiot, Gripper!" retorted Gruff, strongly resenting the insinuation.

"Thank you. You'll see. He *is*, as sure as sure can be. He is putting you in her to give you a benefit—and bring you to your senses."

"I think so too," said Harry Vane. "Squire Jones has been so averse to the sea for Gruff all along."

"It won't do it, then!" cried Mr Gruff in a heat. "You are an idiot too, Vane. I'd as soon go in a trading sloop as I'd go in the biggest naval ship afloat."

"Seven decks and no bottom," put in Gripper.

"You are a jackass, Gripper!" returned Gruff, improving upon his compliments and chafing considerably. "What does it matter how you go to sea, provided you do go? The struggle is to get there at all, when all one's folks are set dead against it."

"Yes, that's it," acquiesced a voice hitherto silent. It was that of William Allair. He sat with his face eagerly raised, his cheeks hectic, his eyes bright. To hear that Gruff Jones was actually going, seemed to speak of hope for himself.

"Look here, Gruff," resumed Gripper, who had seen a good deal of ships at sea and in harbour; the reason possibly why the sea fever had not infected him. "Joking apart, they are wretched, comfortless things, those trading vessels. All hands have to work, and work alike. Nine times out of ten they are imperfectly manned."

"I don't care how much I work."

"You have never tried work yet."

"And what do you mean by 'imperfectly manned?'" pursued Gruff, resentfully.

"Why, suppose the complement of men necessary to work a vessel is, say, fifteen," explained Gripper; "she'll put to sea with only ten or so, boys included. A nice treat that, for the lot! They have to be at work pretty well night and day."

"What fun!" cried Gruff. "I shall like it. Arms were made for work."

"Gripper's saying it out of envy, Gruff," interposed William Allair. "Because he is not going himself."

"It's nothing else," assented Gruff.

Gripper laughed good-humouredly. "I wouldn't make the sea my profession if you paid me in gold to do it. Vane knows I would not. Nobody ever heard me speak up for the sea. If Gruff goes, he'll wish himself back again. Speak the truth, Vane: won't he have a sickener?"

"It's awfully hard work on some of those trading

ships," acknowledged Harry Vane. " Sometimes, too, the treatment's bad. It depends a good deal upon the mate you get."

" The captain, you mean, Vane," said Allair.

" I mean the mate. He has more to do with the apprentice boys than the captain has. You will be sure to have enough of it, Gruff, any way."

" That's first-rate, Vane! *you* talking of hard work at sea," spoke up an incredulous boy : and vastly incredulous they all were, as to there being anything of consequence to do on board a ship. " You have said, hundreds of times, that you did not care what amount of work you should have to do at sea."

" *I* don't," said Harry Vane. " Work does not come amiss to me, be it ever so laborious. Gruff's made of different metal. So is Allair."

" What's that ?" cried William, in a fiery tone.

" So you are," said Gripper. " Vane's right. You are no more fit to go to sea than a girl. As to Gruff, he is the eldest son, and drops into a fortune by inheritance. If ever some of us are to count enough fortune to get bread and cheese, we must work for it. But I'd not work at sea. Some of these days, when Gruff has to heave at the winch, and his arms are aching like mad, and the sweat's pouring off him in bucketfuls, and he knows by experience that it's nothing but work, work, work, from the vessel's starting from one port till she puts into another—a species of Ixion's wheel, you know, which he must be always turning—then he'll say to himself, ' What a fool I was to come here, when I might be at home enjoying myself, and doing nothing!' "

" That's true," nodded Harry Vane.

The boys stared in surprise, Gruff Jones in particular.
" What has come to you, Vane?" he asked. " You
are always preaching up for the sea. Why turn against
it now? I'd never be a turncoat!"

" No fear of my turning against it," replied Harry
Vane. " It is a glorious life, better than any other in
the world, and I hope it will be mine. But I am not
such a daft as to hug myself with the idea that there'll
be nothing to do. You were talking about traders:
well, I know that at sea the work's never done in
them. I shall like the life, even if I go in a trader.
But some of you would not."

" That's all brag," cried Gruff Jones. " We shall
like it as well as you. Why shouldn't we?"

Harry Vane bent over his exercise again. Where
was the use of talking further?

" I say, Gripper, what's the winch for?" resumed
Gruff. " What do they want with a winch on board
ship?"

" You'll find out soon enough, if you go in a trader,"
returned Gripper, with a laugh.

" *If* I go!" ironically retorted Gruff. " As if anything should stop me now!"

" Everybody's not obliged to go in a trader," said
William Allair.

" Not obliged; true," assented Gripper. " Jones
has just told us he's going in one; and all you fellows
who intend running away can't expect anything else.
It's only those nasty dirty traders who look at runaway
chaps. But, go in any ship you will, you'll find the
work enough."

" Keep your ridicule to yourself, Gripper," advised Gruff Jones. " I shall go, in spite of the work."

There is no one thing that boys, having had no experience of a sea life, are, as a rule, so incredulous about, as that there is much work to be done at sea. " What's the work at sea?" said Gruff, scornfully and incredulously. " I shall go, in spite of the work."

And accordingly young Mr Gruff, the squire in embryo, did go. Preliminaries were arranged, the outfit was provided, and the gentleman was conducted by his father on board the trading sloop, spoken of, and commenced his voyage to the Mauritius.

CHAPTER VIII.

On the day that Squire Jones returned to Whittermead, from seeing his son on board, he encountered Mr Allair.

"So you are back, squire," cried Mr Allair, as he shook hands. "And is Hugh actually off?"

"Actually and truly," replied Squire Jones. "I'd have put him downright before the mast, but for the bad companionship of the sailors. As it is, I expect he will get too much of that. But there's no help for it. He must take his chance."

"I suppose he must."

"He'll have to labour with the lowest of them. It is the only way to deal with a boy who gets the sea fever into him: let him go, and work it out. Hugh has no more genuine liking or adaptation for that sort of life than I have. And that he will find out before he is much older."

"He will come back thankful enough to settle down into a quiet country life," remarked Mr Allair.

"Just so; that's why I have sent him. I can't think what possesses the boys to suffer these wild notions to enter their heads," exclaimed Squire Jones, in a tone of vexation. "There's your son; he's another, I hear."

" It arises partly from indolence, partly from a love of roving inherent in some boys, chiefly from a mistaken notion of a sea life. At least, I set it down to those causes," continued Mr Allair. "They see a pretty little skiff gliding on the calm waters of a lake—bask in her themselves, possibly, in the pleasant inertness of a summer's day; and they pick up their notion of life on board ship from that, assuming that the one must be as easy and delightful as the other. A more agreeable mode of spending their time, they think, than working with the hands or the brain, on land."

" That is precisely it," remarked the squire. " Any way, I expect Master Hugh will get enough of it before he is back."

Nothing occurred after this for some little time, worthy of being recorded. The school had dispersed for the summer holidays, always held late at Dr Robertson's, and the boys were enjoying them, while Master Gruff Jones was enjoying the benefit of his chosen voyage.

One morning Mr and Mrs Vane were seated at breakfast, Caroline and Harry with them. Frederick was not back yet: apparently he was finding a London life agreeable.

A servant came in with the letters. There were two: both of them for Mr Vane. One of them he opened in some hurry, glanced over its contents, and put it away in his pocket.

" That letter has an official look," remarked Mrs Vane to him. " Who is it from ?"

Mr Vane controlled a smile, and answered, somewhat evasively. " It is on business."

Harry swallowed his breakfast in haste, and then rose. The summer holidays are a glorious time, boys think, when they have their liberty throughout the sunny day.

"Where are you off to, Harry?"

"Out fly-fishing, papa. I and Allair are going to see if we can't get some fish out of that lazy stream. Gripper said he'd come too, if he could. But we were not to wait for him."

"Will you defer your expedition for an hour?"

Harry scarcely understood. "Allair's waiting for me, papa. I said I'd be with him by nine o'clock."

"Nevertheless, when I request you to wait a little, I suppose you can?"

"Oh, of course, papa," replied Harry, in a cheerful, ready tone of acquiescence. With all his carelessness, he was a thoroughly obedient, right-minded boy.

You can run to Allair's, and tell him that you cannot start just yet. Then come back again."

"Very well," said Harry. "Do you want me to go out for you, papa?"

"All in good time. You will see what I want by and by."

Harry tossed on his cap, and departed. They saw him careering down the road, whistling, leaping, shouting, as healthy boys are given to do. Mr Vane waited until Caroline left the room, and then turned to his wife, speaking somewhat abruptly.

"The time has come when something must be decided about Harry. Sea, or not sea? Which is it to be?"

"Frederick, why do you ask me?"

" Because it rests with you. He has decided to go
to sea, ourselves permitting it. My consent is ready.
What of yours? If you object, something else must
be thought of for him."

Mrs Vane leaned her head upon her hand, sighing
deeply. " I suppose I must say that my consent is also
ready," she presently said, lifting her face and its sad
expression. " I cannot conceal from myself that Harry
appears to be fitted for the sea far more than he is
fitted for any home occupation; and I have latterly
been bringing my mind to contemplate it as a thing
that will be."

" You are doing wisely, Anne," said Mr Vane.

" I consent, out of regard to his wishes—his happiness. He says he could not be happy on land."

" Harry would like your approbation better than
your bare consent," returned Mr Vane, with a smile.
He had always believed it would come to this.

" He shall have it," said Mrs Vane. " If he does go,
he shall not go in a half-and-half way. I can no longer
blind myself to the fact—to the belief, I should rather
say—that it is the sphere where his talents will find
their proper vent; and therefore my duty is plain.
Harry shall go : and may God speed him !"

" I have never understood the ground of your antipathy, Anne," remarked Mr Vane.

" The danger. Nothing else. On board a ship there
will be but a plank between him and eternity."

" Yes, there will : God's protecting hand. The same
God who has watched over and taken care of him on
land, will watch over and protect him on the waters."

" Yes, yes, I know, I know," she reverently answered

F

" But "—after a pause—" we do hear continually of fearful and fatal shipwrecks."

" I cannot deny it. Let us hope that a better fate may be his. Though, when a lad embraces the sea as his occupation, he must be worse than thoughtless if he does not remember that he also embraces its dangers. My father passed his years at sea, and he lived to a good old age, Anne."

" Ay," replied Mrs Vane, who appeared buried in inward thought.

" What is the matter ? You look vexed."

" I am taking blame to myself," she answered, with a half smile. " I might have foreseen that this would be the ending. In fact, I did foresee it: and yet I kept thrusting the thought away from me. I ought to have looked it fully in the face, and allowed proper measures to be taken."

" What do you mean by proper measures ?"

" Yes, I have foreseen it, almost from the boy's infancy," she continued, as if she heard not Mr Vane's question. " Much as I disliked the idea of it myself, there was always a conviction in my inmost heart, a hidden voice, that would now and then make itself heard in spite of me, whispering that the sea would eventually be Harry's destination. It was this silent conviction that kept me from ever saying, ' You shall not go. I will never consent.' My opposition to it has always been a negative one."

" Of which Master Harry has not failed to hold cognisance. He has repeatedly said, ' Mamma has never said I shall not go.' But you were speaking of taking proper measures."

" Of their not having been taken," corrected Mrs Vane. " And I say that I blame myself. Had I summoned up the courage to look at it in the proper light, he might have been entered for the navy. Of course it is too late to do it now, and the merchant service alone is open to him."

Mr Vane laughed. " Well, I had the courage," he said, taking a letter from his pocket, and throwing it upon the table. " Harry has been entered for the navy long ago, and this letter contains his appointment."

Mrs Vane could not immediately take in the sense of the words. " Entered for the navy long ago !" she ejaculated. " Harry ?"

" Even so. I foresaw that the sea would inevitably, humanly speaking, be his destination, and I caused his name to be entered. Had you declined to allow him to depart, the appointment would have been returned, and no harm done."

" I am so glad to hear it !" exclaimed Mrs Vane. " You smile ! You are thinking how suddenly I have veered round in my opinions ! But I assure you there is no suddenness in it. I have been, as I tell you, for some time making my mind up to the unavoidable necessity. And it is the doing so which has, I believe, in a measure, reconciled me to it."

" You will be quite reconciled in time," said Mr Vane.

" Yes, I make no doubt of it. I must trust him to God."

They waited somewhat impatiently for Harry to enter. Mr Vane slowly paced the carpet of the break-

fast room. Mrs Vane sat in deep thought. Presently
he came flying in, eyes bright, cheeks glowing. "Now,
papa?"

Mr Vane wheeled round. " You are soon back, Mr
Midshipman."

The words, the meaning tone, sent the hopeful blood
coursing to the boy's heart. "Papa! Why do you
call me that?"

"Would you like to serve her Majesty, and do
brave battle with her enemies, if called upon?"

"Do you mean to say that I am going into the
navy?" asked Henry, his eagerness great.

"Did you notice that I received a large letter this
morning?—your mamma remarked that it had an official look."

"Yes—yes!"

"It contained your appointment. Harry Vane, Midshipman, R.N. How do you like the sound?"

Harry turned his eyes upon his mother. His father
was laughing, his tone a joking one altogether; nevertheless he believed the truth the words conveyed. But
what of his mother?

The tears stood in her eyes as she held out her hand
to him. "I have consented, Harry."

"Oh, mamma! How shall I ever thank you?"

"By being still my own noble boy, dutiful and good,
although you are away from me."

"I will try to be. Papa, what ship am I commis-
sioned to? Do I join at once?"

"Hark at the impatience!" exclaimed Mr Vane, in
a mock serious tone. "Why don't you ask, young
gentleman, what ship will have the honour of carrying

your flag? You must undergo a nice little course of study first, sir: instead of joining a ship, you join the naval college, and fag for your examination. In six months' time you may think about a ship—if you are lucky."

"All right!" cried Harry, heartily. "I'll fag; fag with the best of them. What do you think I have been doing, papa?"

"Many things that you ought not, I expect."

"I daresay I have," honestly confessed Harry. "But I have been studying navigation. I have indeed, papa, all my spare time. I got the books out of Robertson's library, and I shouldn't be afraid now to navigate a ship with any captain going."

Mr Vane burst into a laugh. "That is modest, Harry, at any rate."

"Well, papa, it seems to come to me by intuition. Gruff Jones thought he'd have a go in at it; and he did, and was tired in a week. Horrid stuff, he called it; as dry as sawdust."

Mr Vane left the room, laughing still. Harry turned to his mother.

"Mamma, why is it that you have always, until now, so disliked the idea of my going to sea?"

"Your papa has just asked me nearly the same question. I answer you as I answered him. The danger, Harry! Have you ever reflected that on board ship there will be but a plank between you and eternity?"

Harry looked a shade graver than usual. His countenance brightened as he hastened to reply:

"There's no real danger on board one of her Majesty's ships, mamma. They never get drowned—as the children say. I hope I shall be appointed to a three-decker! They are well built, well manned, and their strength is our protection."

"What else do you think is your protection?" quietly rejoined Mrs Vane.

He made no reply: though quite conscious what she meant.

"When I spoke to your papa of the danger, my boy, he reminded me that the same God who has hitherto watched over you on the land, will watch over you on the sea. Ah, Harry! you talk of the ship's strength being your protection. What protection could there be in a few frail boards, unless He held them together?"

"Mamma, I was speaking only of man's strength."

"I know. Listen to me, darling. The sea *is* a hazardous life, more so than common: take you heed, therefore, that you abide always under God's good care. Morning after morning, night after night, commit yourself to Him. Never omit it; never forget it. *Try and find God.* Try and realize the fact that He is ever present with you, your powerful Protector, so long as you trust to Him. Amidst the hurry and bustle of a sea life, steal a moment sometimes for Him; in the silent deck watches, let your heart be often lifted up to Him. Trust yourself wholly to God: let your ever-recurring daily prayer be, 'Lord, my time is in Thy hand: do Thou undertake for me!' And then you may rest assured that, whether He shall see fit to spare you, or to take you, it must, and will, be for the best. Do you think you can realize this, Harry?"

"I can hope for it," he answered.

"Hope and strive. Your prayers will not ascend

alone. For every one that you breathe, I shall offer up its fellow. It is a pleasant belief, that which some of our divines have given utterance to—that the urgent prayers of a mother for her child are never lost. Void they may be, for a time—dormant the answer may seem to lie: but the fruit appears at last. I often think that no prayers can be so urgently fervent, as those sent up by a mother for her boy at sea."

"What was it papa wanted with me?" inquired Harry, after a pause, turning to a lighter subject.

"To inform you of the news; and to let you know that you would have but a few days longer at Whittermead. You may go on your fishing expedition now."

CHAPTER IX.

THE fishing expedition, all-important as it was before, had faded into nothingness. What was that trifling pastime in comparison with these great tidings? Boiling over with excitement, scarcely knowing whether he stood on his head or his heels, Harry Vane hunted out his glazed sailor's hat—the article he had invested a certain Christmas-box in the previous Christmas—and proceeded to the linen-draper's shop. There he went in trust for four yards of blue ribbon, wound it round his hat, leaving the ends flying, and proceeded to show himself in the village. "I am going to sea! I am going at last!" was his salute to everybody. At length he reached Mr Allair's.

"Give me joy, William!" he cried, bursting in, and waving his hat in triumph. "The long lane has at length had a turning."

"What on earth do you mean?" asked William Allair, staring at the ribbons.

"I am off in a few days; off to Woolwich, or some of those places, and in six months join the navy—the best middy it ever had, if it will only appreciate me."

"You have gone deranged, I think."

"It's with joy, then. Why, I am telling you nothing but sober fact. The governor—like a sensible governor that he is—entered my name for the navy long ago, though he never spoke of it; and to-day my appointment arrived. Of course he had to speak of it then."

"In the navy!" repeated William, rather overwhelmed with the news that had broken upon him.

"Is it not prime? I had made up my mind, if I did get to sea, to have a hard working life of it, on board some obscure trader perhaps,—like Gruff Jones's,—and now there's this glorious prospect opened to me. Oh, I am so heartily glad! I shall be as happy as the days are long."

William sighed a sigh of envy. "But what will Mrs Vane say?" he questioned.

"She is a dear mother, and has shown out sensible too. She says it is evidently my appointed sphere of usefulness in life; and so she'll oppose it no longer, but send me away with a God speed."

"Well, I'm sure I wish other mothers and people would show out sensible," cried poor William—discontent and envy uncommonly rife in his heart just then. "What have you tied those blue things round your hat for?"

"To let the public in general know of my luck," said Harry, with a laugh. "I shall hang a flag out at my bed-room window when I get home. I say, I am in no mood for fishing to-day. I must race about to spread the news—going to Lady Sayingham first. I know she'll be glad."

"Who cares for fishing?" returned William. "I don't. I don't mind if I never go fishing again. I wish I was you, Vane! Some people do get all the luck of it in this world."

Harry Vane laughed good-naturedly. "Never was such luck as mine."

"Well, this is a change!" repeated William. "Why, it was only yesterday you were saying your hope of sea was further off than ever."

"I thought it was. But, look you, I did not despair of going some time or other."

"Suppose they had still held out against it—your father and Mrs Vane—what should you have done? Run away?"

"What rubbish! Gruff Jones asked me that, one day. As if I should take the reins into my own hands in that way! No good comes of defying your father, when they are good fathers, you know, as ours are. Besides, it's not gentlemanly to play the runagate."

"Then what *should* you have done," persisted William, "supposing they had held out in denying you the sea?"

"Stopped on land, and made the best of it, always hoping that something or other would turn up to subdue their prejudices. I did not think my mother would come-to, yet awhile, at any rate; and I never would have gone in opposition to her. She is my mother, you know, Allair, and a regular good mother, too; and I'd not have turned against her. I shall look out for luck and happiness now. And that's what I never should have had, if I had gone in opposition to my mother."

William sat drumming on the table. "I wish fathers and mothers could see with our eyes!" he impulsively cried.

"I had been casting about in my mind what I could do—what employment would be the least distasteful to me, hopes of the sea being at a discount," went on

Harry. "And I had nearly fixed on being a ship's carpenter."

"A ship's carpenter!" repeated William, in astonishment.

"In some of our great big dockyards," he continued, with equanimity. "A ship's carpenter, or ship-builder, —anything of that. It would have brought me into constant contact with ships; and that's the next best thing to sailing in them."

"But to be a ship's carpenter! That's such hard work!"

"Well, a builder, then. But what do I care for hard work? Knocking about suits me. And, as I tell you, I should always have had the hope upon me that some lucky turn-up would send me to sea. But, I say, Allair, what a stunning thing it is that I have got on so far with navigation! I *would* stick to that; and I *did*. Ha, ha! that's of more use to me than Latin and Greek. I'll leave the classics to you—you'll want them. William Allair, Esquire, attorney-at-law, and one of the Masters Extraordinary in the High Court of Chancery! *Exempli gratiâ!*"

Catching up his hat, with a joyous, ringing laugh, Harry Vane tossed it on his head sideways, sailor fashion, and tore away towards Sayingham Court, his blue streamers flying behind him.

William remained alone, giving way to one of the most discontented reveries he had ever had the pleasure of indulging. It showed itself in his countenance. He carried his gloomy looks into the presence of his mother.

"What can be the matter?" she exclaimed, as soon as she caught sight of his face.

"Harry Vane's going to sea."

Mrs Allair was surprised at the answer. "To sea! Well, need you look so sorrowful over it? He will be home occasionally, I suppose."

"Who's looking sorrowful over that?" not very dutifully responded William; but he was in a testy temper. "I wish I could go with him! That's why I look sorrowful: because I want to go, and can't."

Mrs Allair laughed pleasantly. "Don't envy him, William. You will find happiness in a home life—he in a sea one."

"Mr and Mrs Vane have consented, have approved. It turns out that he was entered for the navy long ago, and now his appointment's come," continued William, in a tone of fierce resentment against things in general.

"I am glad to hear it: glad that Mrs Vane has seen for the best at last. Were Harry Vane my boy, I believe I should have seen it long ago."

"That's good, mother!" retorted William; "when you know how you hate the sea."

"I don't hate it; you are mistaken. What would become of our ships, our commerce, our prosperity, our proud name as mistress of the world, if there were to be no sailors?"

"I am sure you hate it for me."

"That is another thing. Though 'hate' is not precisely the right word."

"You and Mrs Vane both hate the sea like poison," persisted William, who was not in a conciliatory mood. "At least, she has hated it up to now; and it's odd to me, what has changed her," he added, *par parenthèse*. "Were it the river Styx, you could neither of you

have gone on more against it. Do you remember the
duet you kept up, the last time we were at the Vanes'
at tea?"

"Our 'going on,' as you call it, has arisen from
different motives," said Mrs Allair. "Mrs Vane dislikes a sea life in itself. She dislikes it for its hazards,
its dangers — dislikes to live a life of almost constant
separation from her son : hence has arisen her opposition to Harry's embracing it. My objection is a different one. I dislike it *for you*, because I know how
entirely unfitted you are for it, both in temperament
and physical capacity. Were you constituted as Harry
Vane is, you should go with pleasure."

"Where's the difference between one boy and another?" debated William, who of course was seeing
things through his own one-sided spectacles. "There's
none."

Mrs Allair quite laughed at the words. "So much
difference is there, William, that what would be pastime
to one boy would kill another. Do you suppose that
all are endowed alike?—equally strong to endure the
rubs and crosses of life?"

"Well, it's not very kind of you, mamma, to preach
up for Harry Vane, and ridicule me."

"When boys fall into an absurd temper, the best
plan is to let them alone until they fall out of it again,"
said Mrs Allair, still good-humouredly. "Be reason-
able, William. There has been no preaching for Harry
Vane, except in saying that he is fitted for a sea life ;
and there has certainly been no ridicule cast upon you.
You have each your several and individual talents.
Never was a boy more suited to a profession than you

are to follow that of your father: but were Harry Vane
to attempt to follow it, he would break down. You are
adapted for one sphere; he for another. The prospect
of making it your pursuit in life afforded you pleasure
at one time."

" That was before I knew anything about the sea."

" Allow me to ask you a question, William—if you
can for a moment get the sea out of your head. Were
you left at liberty to choose your profession, is not that
of a solicitor the one you would prefer?"

" I would prefer going to sea."

" I asked you to put the sea out of your head for an
instant. I speak of life on land. Answer me."

" Well, I'd as soon be a lawyer as anything else.
Rather, I think. There's no hard work in it."

" Yes, I knew it. You have no dislike to the calling,
in itself, but the contrary; and you are well adapted
for it. But in this wild notion that you have taken up,
and persist in encouraging, you lose sight of things
fitting. I can only compare you to a blind man,
William—one who has taken a wrong turning, and
gropes his way along in darkness, believing he is on
the right road, whereas each step takes him farther
from his destination."

" The world calls all lawyers rogues," cried dutiful
William.

Mrs Allair turned her eyes gravely upon him.
" William!"

The boy blushed at the silent reproof. It was very
like an insult to his father's name, and he wished he
had not spoken it.

" All lawyers are not rogues," pursued Mrs Allair,

quietly. " Some are honest and honourable, even in the sight of men; striving earnestly to do right before God. William, *you know* that your father is one of these."

" I know he is. Indeed, mamma, when I spoke, I was not thinking of him."

" And you can be one of these honourable men, if you will. A profession or a trade is just what its exerciser makes it; one of honour, or one of shame. The highest calling in life is that of a minister of God; and yet, William, we know how some, professing it, have made it a disgrace."

" I wish I was in Harry Vane's shoes—going to sea," ejaculated William, reverting to the old grievance. " I shouldn't disgrace that. Seymour must hand over his wager, now."

" What wager?" asked Mrs Allair.

" Oh, he laid a bet with young Robertson. There was a talk in the school—knowing how his going to sea was objected to at home—as to whether Vane wouldn't take French leave, and run away. Seymour bet he would——"

" William!"

The interrupting word was spoken in a tone of painful wailing. William looked up in surprise. Every vestige of colour had forsaken his mother's cheek, and she gazed at him with a yearning look of apprehension. Had a prophetic vision of the future come across her?

" Why, mamma, what's the matter?"

" I do not like to hear such things spoken. Wicked ideas they are, William. Had Harry Vane taken so false a step, it would have killed his mother."

" Killed her!" echoed William.

" It surely would. Were my darling boy"—she laid her hand impressively upon his shoulder—" my best and dearest son, ever to fall into so terrible an act of disobedience, it would kill me. Not at once; no: but, if I know anything of myself, the sorrow would bring me to a lingering death. It must be a grievous thing, William, to die of a broken heart," she added, with a shiver.

" Mamma, what *are* you saying!"

" I think I could bear any sorrow better than the rebellion of my children. Not for my sake; no, no. I could struggle with the trouble it might bring to me; but I could not bear it for them. Nothing but sorrow could be in store for them, if they so set at defiance the law of God. For every pain a child feels, its mother undergoes one infinitely greater. She suffers in and for her children. Many a mother has been laid in her grave by the ungrateful conduct of her sons. William, take you care never so to offend, if you would have God's blessing rest upon you."

William was softened to contrition. " You cannot fear such a step for me, mamma!"

" My boy, I would almost rather die than fear it! I do not fear it."

" You never shall have cause," whispered William. He spoke in his earnest belief: and the tears shone in his eyes as he fondly kissed his mother.

A few days, and Harry Vane departed. The whole village was sad, for he was a favourite with everybody; but none were more sad than William Allair. Not that he was grieving after Harry Vane, personally:

boys are not so sentimental. His grief lay chiefly for himself: because he was not going; or, so far as he saw, likely to go.

"This is obstinacy, William," said Mr Allair, hearing a rebellious and discontented speech that William gave utterance to. "You must let your good sense return to you, or you will seriously displease me."

"We can't help our likes and dislikes, papa."

"We can *persuade* ourselves into any liking or disliking that we choose," significantly rejoined Mr Allair; "especially when we turn obstinate over it. You have picked up this very absurd fancy about the sea, and are hugging it and cherishing it by every means in your power. Take care that it does not over-master you, so as to render you permanently dissatisfied and miserable. Put it away from you, William. It is good advice, mind, that I give you."

"Of course you think it is, papa."

"And you don't," said Mr Allair. He never supposed this fancy of William's would turn out to be a serious one, or that they should have trouble over it. "William," he resumed, in a joking tone, "my old uncle was very fond of repeating a certain truth to us boys, wishing it to be impressed upon our memory. 'Young folks think old folks fools; but the old folks know the young ones to be so.'"

"What a donkey the old fellow must have been!" thought William.

CHAPTER X.

THE time went on. Harry Vane, in due course, joined the "Hercules," Captain Stafford, as midshipman, and the ship departed on what was thought would prove a long cruise.

There was a spirit of obstinacy in William Allair, not altogether pleasant. Did he set his mind upon a thing and get opposed, so much the more eager became he for it, simply because he *was* opposed. Mr Allair's remark, that we can persuade ourselves into any liking or disliking that we choose, was a perfectly correct one. Boys, take you notice of this. When you are earnestly bent upon some project, some idea, and protest that you cannot get it out of your head, such hold has it there, although you know (if you listen to your conscience) that it ought to be got out, just try and discover whether the fault does not lie with you. You are prejudiced in its favour; you look at it but from one point of view; you think, there it is in your head, and there it must be, and all your efforts tend to keep it there. Suppose you were to try the opposite course; to make a few genuine efforts to throw it away, instead of to keep it; you might find the benefit. So great is this prejudice carried, that a boy may set on and long for the moon; ay, and may grow ill, miserable, feverish, because he can't get it. But were the coveted thing thrown into his lap—the moon, or any other toy so wished for—he might find it a source of pain, instead of pleasure; a subject for loathing, rather than for liking.

It was just so with William Allair. You have seen that he had set his mind upon going to sea; and although he promised his mother he would no longer think of it, the desire continued in all its unabated force. He tried no means, save wrong ones, to make good his promise. Instead of striving manfully to put the wish from him, he took all possible pains to augment it. The appetite grows by what it feeds on. He so fed this ideal desire, that it was becoming nearly irrepressible. Never once did he say to himself, "I will turn my thoughts away from its fascinations." All his wishes were on the wrong side, and pursued in a spirit of discontent. "How I wish I could go! What a shame it is of them to deny me! As if they could tell what I should like to be, so well as I can!" After this fashion did the gentleman daily and hourly reason.

Harry Vane's final departure, in high glowing spirits, had tended to fan the flame. Before he joined the "Hercules," he came home for a few days; and his golden visions, breathed in William's hearing, of the stirring life he was about to enter on, excited William beyond everything. He grew pining, moping, miserable; quite unhappy.

And so had passed the months: autumn, winter, spring; and summer came round again and was quickly flitting.

Dr Robertson's school broke up for the summer holidays. William quitted it for good, and was very shortly to be articled to his father. But about this time, as ill luck would have it, there arrived a young man at Whittermead on a visit to the Jennikers. His name was Carter, and he was related to Mrs Jenniker. He was a sailor, second mate of an Indiaman, of which vessel his father was captain and part owner.

Young Carter had seen only the more favourable auspices of a sea life. Voyaging with and under his father, in a fine vessel, well disciplined, well provisioned, accustomed to the sea from boyhood—for he had more than once been taken the voyage to India for pleasure—possessing also a natural liking for it, there is no wonder that he spoke of it in terms of enthusiasm. He had nearly as great a liking for it as had Harry Vane. With this gentleman William became intimate, and it was productive to him of much mischief.

William imparted to him his longing for the sea. Mr Carter, fond of boasting, proud of speaking well of his own pursuit in life, encouraged the longing. He pictured a sea life in colours so glowing, that one, with less inclination for it than William, might well have been taken in. His own good sense ought to have told him that James Carter had seen only the bright side of the profession; and all professions have two sides, a bright and a dark one. Sometimes the dark becomes bright, and the bright dark, according as the eyes of the regarders view them. Three weeks did the visit of Mr Carter last: three pernicious weeks to William Allair. He had dwelt a vast deal too much upon going to sea before; but now he dwelt upon it in a different spirit. Then he had said, "I wish I could go:" now he began to say, "I will go."

His entire conversation now, whether with young Carter or others, was of the sea. His thoughts by day never quitted it; at night his dreams brought it to him again. You may perceive that he never attempted *not* to think of it; he encouraged his mind to dwell upon it; and therein lay his error.

At home he said nothing; he had given over speaking of it to his father and mother.

A hint had been imparted to William of the disease that threatened his father—that he could look for no long life. It was Mrs Allair who had told him; and hence it was so necessary that he—he, William—should be rendered capable of taking to the business in his father's place. But the impression made upon him at the time by this communication had worn away. He was sure his father was not ill, he reasoned with himself. He was active, and lively, and looked well— why shouldn't he live as long as other people? As for himself, he should get plenty of money at sea. Sailors, especially when they got to be mates, had good pay; and captains always made money; some of them were as rich as Crœsus. Oh, yes, he should fill his pockets with money there, and he'd bring every farthing of it home to his dear mother.

Somewhat after this fashion did William constantly reason. His mind was unsettled, his brain was at work, his heart was miserable. The first day that he was to take his place in his father's office happened to be the day fixed for James Carter's departure from Whittermead. At half-past nine, the usual hour of Mr Allair's proceeding to his office, he looked into a room that his children were fond of sitting in.

" Come, William."

" I'll follow you, papa. I'll be there as soon as you are." But the words were not spoken cheerfully or readily.

He took his hat, however, and went out after his father. It was a warm, beautiful day—too warm; inclining idle people to idleness. William, as a matter of course, began wishing that he could go roaming about the fields, instead of being cooped up in a close room, and—worse thought still!—where he was to be cooped up for ever so many years to come. In the midst of his murmurs, an open carriage came bowling towards him. It contained Mr Jenniker and James Carter, the latter being driven to the four-mile-off station to catch the London train. James Carter, who had previously taken leave, moved his hat in an animated manner to William.

" Yes! he may well look pleased," grumbled William, as he turned to gaze after the carriage. " He is going to enjoy the beauty of this sunny day, while I must be stewed to death in that horrible old office. Put Carter into one, and see whether he'd stand it! And next week he sets sail for China! It's a shame there should be so much disparity in the world!"

In this remarkably cordial mood did William take his appointed place on the high stool at the clerk's desk, and begin the work assigned him. It was the copying of a deed. But now we all know how unpalatable—nay, how almost unbearable—is a task to which we set ourselves unwillingly. With every word that William wrote, his eyes were raised to the dusky panes of the window opposite him. A wretchedly discontented feeling filled his mind. He was longing to be careering abroad in that bright sunshine, or to be basking idly beside some gleaming pond; in short, to be doing anything but what he was doing.

The day seemed a terribly long one, and his task irksome to a degree—as was sure to be the case, pursuing it with so ill a will. Had it been the most delightful employment, he would, in his present temper, have completed it rebelliously. He set himself against it. Every line that he wrote chafed his spirit worse than the preceding one; and, at length, it was with difficulty that he could bring himself or his fingers to go on with it at all. Like an idle child, who is put to learn a lesson when he would rather play, the closer he is kept to his task, the more impatient and fretful does he become. William Allair was like too many of you. How often are you discontented with the task assigned you, and get through it perforce, your unwilling spirit bubbling up to rebellion! You think the fault lies in the work—that it is irksome beyond bearing, flat, stale, unprofitable; everything that the English language can express of bad. But you are mistaken; the fault is in *you*. Throw your antipathy to the winds; return to it with a willing mind, a cheerful spirit, and you will find its irksomeness gone. William Allair had not the sense to do this.

At five o'clock, and in a very ill humour, he left the office for the day. Contrasting, as he went along, the dull employment he had been kept to, with the delight of a sail over the dark blue waters—as Mr James Carter was wont to style the sea. They are green sometimes, though, mind you, and very angry. Upon

entering home, his brother Edmund came dancing gleefully about him, holding something concealed in his
hand. "It's for you," said Edmund, with his vacant
laugh. "Guess."

"Don't tease, Edmund," was the fretful answer. "I
am too tired to guess. Keep it yourself."

"Tired, are you?" asked Mrs Allair.

"Just dead," groaned William.

"But what has so tired you?"

"Why, the writing, of course. Write, write, write
all day—the pen going upon one parchment, and the
eyes upon another. I feel quite ill. I am convinced I
can't stand it long."

"You will soon get used to it."

"I shall never get used to it. And I shall never like it."

"Not if you set your mind against it, as I fear you
are doing," replied Mrs Allair. She need not have said,
"I fear:" it was all too plain. William was allowing this
discontent to take entire possession of him; making his
mind unhappy, souring his temper. He loved his mother
beyond everything in life; but he was losing sight both
of love and duty in this unhappy state of feeling.

"How hot it has been to-day!" exclaimed William.
"Too hot to stop in-doors, unless you are forced to it."

"I always thought out of doors was hotter than in,
in the extreme summer weather," remarked Mrs Allair.
"Where is your papa?" she added. "The dinner is
waiting."

"He is coming soon, I suppose," ungraciously rejoined
William.

"Edmund is holding a letter for you. It is from
Harry Vane. They received a packet from him to-day,

and Caroline brought yours up.   He is well and happy.
The one he wrote to her she read aloud to us.   Edmund,
give it to your brother."

William tore open the letter, glanced at its contents,
swallowed down his dinner at a speed enough to choke
him, and then went to his own room, to digest the
letter at leisure.   But it had come at a most unlucky
time, filled, as it was, with a seductive description of
Harry Vane's sea life, painted in accordance with his
peculiar temperament, his highly-wrought imagination.
He had not deceived himself; his satisfaction in it was
as great as he had expected it would be; and he expressed his regret that William was not with him; or,
at any rate, on board a ship of some sort.   He said he
had been in a storm at sea; that no description could
do justice to its terrific grandeur, and that he had felt
subdued and awe-struck, but never for one instant
alarmed.   The letter also contained some charming
anecdotes of Madeira—all in midshipman style—and of
other places where they had touched; and it concluded
with the information that the captain was a " stunner,"
and the " grub" good.

William read the letter over and over again.   To his
jaundiced mind, it appeared to contain—that is, the
ship—all that can exist of earthly Elysium.   A dim
thought which had long hovered over his mind, and as
often been thrust away again, came rushing on now
with ominous force.   It brought a hot glow to his face.
He made some resistance to it, for the conscience was at
variance with the will.   But the mental repugnance grew
fainter and fainter; and at length William Allair rose up,
yielding to the temptation, and his fate in life was sealed.

CHAPTER XI.

A RACE WITH A GIG.

It was a battle; but not a great one. Where the wish to do wrong is powerful, and the conscience deadened, resistance does not cost much.

The resolve to run away had come over William Allair. The wicked resolve. He determined to quit his father's house clandestinely, proceed to London or Liverpool, and get himself engaged on board a ship about to sail for some distant port. He leaned his head upon his hand, and thought it over. While he did so, a wavering arose within him, and at the same moment a harsh, discordant noise was heard, as of some bird of prey flying over the house. Why did he not take the ill omen as a warning? He wavered, I say. And then he set himself deliberately to recall Mr Carter's glowing descriptions, his marine tales, and again read Harry Vane's letter: just as though he wished to subdue the wavering. He was deliberating, he thought. But he was deliberating in a partial manner, all the bias leaning to one side. So the faint, still small voice that would have saved him was disregarded; and he rose up with his resolution fixed.

Yet, pause ere you execute it, William Allair! As you value your happiness in this life, and, it may be, in the next, pause! If no other thought can deter you, remember your mother. You were her first-born; you

are dearer to her than any other tie on earth: the love
she bears for you is planted in every fibre of her heart,
is interwoven with her existence. She guarded you in
infancy, watched over you in sickness, soothed you in
your wayward childhood. She has looked at you until
her eyes were dim with tears in her excess of love ; she
has caught you to her bosom, praying that God would
have mercy on you, and keep you in this world and in
the next. When you have been wrathful, when you
have committed faults, and others have chidden, she
has found excuses for you in her heart, loving you all
the more for their harshness. Others may, and do, love
you ; but not as she does. The love of a mother stands
alone ; there is nothing on earth so deep and so holy.

There is no passion, no affection in the whole wide
world of nature, that can be compared in its enduring
strength with that of a mother. A brother loves his
sister, a sister her brother ; a father loves his child, the
child its father ; and there is *another* love spoken of
in the world, William Allair, which it may chance you
will some day experience, but which, all-potent as it is,
cannot stand beside a mother's ; for her love for you will
be green and fresh, when all of that transient one, save
its remembrance, shall have passed away. The heart
of all—father, sister, brother—may grow cold to you ;
but your mother's, never. Shame, poverty, guilt, every
ill that will cause others to shun you, does but draw
closer the love of a mother ; it is the only solace that
will cling to you in your depth of guilt and sorrow.
And you would fly from a shield such as this ? My
boy, in mercy to your mother, desert her not.

Think what you are about to do. To isolate yourself

from her, to leave her to anxiety and despair, ignorant
of your destination, uncertain what your fate may be.
Pause, ere you *thus* requite her love, and embitter her
whole future life with this black ingratitude!

Know you not, that if she could fathom your project,
she would cast herself on her knees before you, and
implore you, with tears and kisses, not to fly from her;
not to turn her tranquil days to one long, bitter, unavailing yearning—the yearning to behold you, her
dearest and best-beloved child? Know you not that,
night and morning, she bends before God in supplication for you, that you may be good, dutiful, kept from
the evil? Know you not that she would rather lose
life in this world, than that you should lose it?

Oh! pause, pause, William Allair! pause, ere you
fling back this all-enduring love! It is a painful thing
to rend a mother's heart; to bring grey hairs upon her
head before their time; to shorten her declining years
of life with anguish. It is a sin that must cry aloud
in its ascent to heaven: pause, ere you are guilty of it!
Have you forgotten that it was she who taught you
certain commandments with her own lips, and bade you
strive to keep them? Have you forgotten this one?
" HONOUR THY FATHER AND THY MOTHER : THAT THY DAYS
MAY BE LONG IN THE LAND WHICH THE LORD THY GOD
GIVETH THEE."

No, you have not forgotten it, William Allair: the
words rush to your mind now, and your conscience
shrinks. But you attempt to make a compromise with
your conscience. You resolve that you will one day
come back to your mother's hearth, at no great distance
of time—when you shall have been over the broad seas,

or to those foreign lands you seem so desirous to visit
—and then you will implore her pardon with tears and
contrition, and be all to her that a son should be.
But does no shadow of the future cross you? does no
suggestion whisper that it is just possible you never
may return? that you may *die* in one of those foreign
lands, or on those broad seas? You will do well to
pause. I tell it you for the last time.

You will not?

Then you must follow your own course. Yet, remember, when you are on the world of waters—when,
as Mrs Vane aptly expressed it, there is only a plank
between you and eternity, and the waves rush, and the
winds shriek around you, and the good ship seems
destined to sink—when you call in anguish upon your
father and mother's name, and would fain implore their
forgiveness before appearing at the bar of a higher
tribunal; remember that it is *you* who have placed
yourself beyond the power of receiving it.

William Allair shook off his reverie, shook off com-
punction with it, unlocked a drawer, and examined his
purse. It contained eighteen shillings. Had it been
Harry Vane's, it would not have contained eighteen
farthings; but William had always been more inclined
to save than to spend.

Mrs Allair also held a sovereign of his. A few days
previously, his uncle had sent him one as a present,
wishing him at the same time joy of his articles.

"He knows they are a bitter pill," was William's
remark at the time.

He tied up a few things in a pocket-handkerchief,
sailor fashion, locked the bundle in a drawer, lest it

should be espied, and went down stairs. The tea-things were on the table, but only his mother and sisters were in the room.

"Mamma, you have a sovereign of mine. The one my uncle sent me. I want it, please."

"Very well. But don't go spending it in waste, William."

"Waste! oh, dear, no. Can you give it me now?"

Alice looked up. "You can't want it now, William: you are not going out. Let mamma give it you at her leisure."

"It is no affair of yours, Alice. Mamma, please! I really do want it."

Mrs Allair laughed, as she rose to get the money. "That you may have the pleasure of seeing it in your own purse," she said, as she handed it to him.

But he was not dead to all feeling. No, no. In spite of the wicked project which occupied his mind, which appeared to him so fraught with glowing colours for the future, he felt miserably wretched. And when his mother bent over him for her good-night kiss, he thought his heart would have broken.

When everybody was at rest, and the house quiet, he opened the door of his chamber to steal down stairs. He stood listening for some moments, and then moved forward. Alice's door was before him, his mother's at the end of the corridor. William could see them, in the faint light that came in from the corridor window, and almost expected them in his self-consciousness to open, and somebody to come out and pounce upon him. Holding by the balustrades when he reached the stairs, he attempted to go a little quicker; but the stairs began to creak alarmingly, and he stood still, his face hot, his breath hushed.

What excuse could he make if he *were* found? He could not offer the plea that he was going for a walk: people don't take walks at midnight, as a matter of choice. He could not say he made a mistake, and got up thinking it was morning: they'd ask him whether he dressed in the dark. And he could not well say he was promenading in his sleep. Mr William Allair's face grew hotter.

But things remained quiet, and he went more slowly, step by step. the stairs creaking dreadfully—just as *you* have found them creak, boys, when wishing to steal up or down unnoticed. Unmolested, he at length gained the street door, and was about to unlock it, when he remembered he had left his bundle behind.

For one single moment the thought came over him, should he relinquish his expedition? Oh that he had! that he had suffered the delay to sway him, to act upon him as an omen!

He crept up stairs again, reached his room, got the bundle, and crept down. This time he opened the door, and got safely out, closing it as softly as possible after him.

There was no moon: but the stars were shining, and the night was warm and light. He stood a moment deliberating upon his course, and then he started. He had resolved to go to Liverpool. Not towards any railway station went he. He was afraid of that, afraid he might be traced; but chose rather bye-roads. The way once chosen, onward he pressed; now walking with rapid strides. now running swiftly, terribly afraid lest he should be missed and overtaken.

Very slowly did the hours of the night seem to pass; and on, went he, putting more distance between himself and Whittermead. "They'll be sure not to miss me before breakfast-time," he kept repeating to himself: but there was an under-current of fear at work within him, whispering that he *might* be missed earlier, and overtaken. He thought the night would never go.

It was just past four in the morning, for William had his watch with him; the sun was rising, and he was pelting along at a fine pace, tired to death; when he heard the sound of wheels behind. Were they after him? One hasty look back, and away he tore as fast as his legs could carry him. Something there was, at a great distance, coming along at a strapping pace; but what, he could not yet discern.

Away he dashed. The vehicle came dashing on faster. William snatched another look, and saw that it was a gig.

A gig! His father's, no doubt. There was no feasible way of escape for William. On either side of the road was a perpendicular embankment, the climbing which was impossible. There was nothing for it but to go blindly on, or to turn back and face the gig.

Another stolen glance. Yes, sure enough, it was their gig, and one gentleman in it: his father, of course. What was he to do? What *was* he to do? William had heard of earthquakes. He began to wish that one would obligingly sever the earth just then, and allow him to drop into the chasm.

On it came at full gallop, he was sure; and on went William at full gallop also: his face streaming down with perspiration, his breath panting. He thought of

Dick Turpin's ride to York, and questioned if the renowned highwayman had ridden faster than *he* was then running.

But he could not keep up the pace, and the gig gained upon him; canter, canter, canter; nearer, nearer, nearer. It was at his heels now; and now—it was abreast of him.

With a desperate effort he turned his face towards it; no good in holding out longer; and there he beheld —what? Why, sufficient to impress fully on his mind the old adage, " Conscience doth make cowards of us all."

It was neither his father, nor his father's gig; but a farmer on his way to a market-town. The stranger accosted him.

" So, young gentleman, you are pretty fast! Why, you weren't afraid of me—eh ?"

" Afraid! oh, no!" panted William, alarmed lest suspicion should be excited. " I am in a hurry, and, seeing your gig coming, I thought I'd have a race with it. It has got me on, you see."

" You have got on, pretty smartly. I have come at a tolerable pace, for I'm later than I thought to be. I am going on to Brickborough, a matter of eleven miles yet. It's the fair there to-day."

Brickborough was the very town William was making for, where he would take the rail. How he wished the farmer would invite him into the gig! " I am going on to Brickborough, too," he said.

The farmer did invite him; perhaps, taking the hint. " Will you accept a seat in my chay?" he asked. " You are heartily welcome to it."

And very welcome, indeed, did it prove to the tired runaway, who parried the farmer's questions cleverly, and arrived safely at Brickborough. Thence he would make his way to Liverpool in the best manner that he could.

" They'll make sure I have gone up to London to join Carter, and will raise the hue-and-cry in that direction," he cogitated, " which will give me time to get clear off on the briny ocean. Ah, ha! I am too deep for them!"

Ah, William! deep and clever as you deem yourself now, the time will come when you would give all your future existence to re-live the period of this ill-starred journey, so that you might have been less "deep," and have suffered yourself to be overtaken!

CHAPTER XII.

WHEN the morning broke at Whittermead, and the Allairs assembled at breakfast, William's place was vacant.

"Lazy boy! he has overslept himself," said Rose.

A servant was placing a dish of toasted bacon on the table. Mrs Allair spoke to her.

"Go up to Master William's room, Sarah. Tell him we are at breakfast."

Sarah went, stayed some minutes, and came back again. "I've knocked till I'm tired, ma'am," said she. "He won't answer."

"Perhaps he is not awake yet," suggested Rose.

"Oh, I know," said Alice. "He thinks that there's no seven o'clock school now, and won't get up. He is sure to be awake; he has allowed Sarah to knock to tease her."

"Go up again, Sarah," said Mrs Allair. "If he does not answer, go into his room. It is possible he may have overslept himself. He said last night he was very tired."

The servant did as she was bid, and the next minute came flying into the room big with excitement, her eyes staring and her mouth open.

"Oh, ma'am! oh, sir! whatever has happened? Master William is not in his room, and the bed has never been slept in! Where can he have took himself to?"

"Nonsense! You must be mistaken, Sarah," spoke Mr Allair. But Mrs Allair turned deadly pale.

"How can I be mistaken, sir? There's the bed for anybody to see. And I am sure he is not in the room."

Alice and Rose Allair ran up the stairs. Mrs Allair followed more slowly; she knew not what she was dreading. Mr Allair came after her. The chamber was empty, as the servant had said. There was no trace of William: no trace that he had been in since the previous evening.

Mrs Allair turned her gaze upon her husband, words faltering from her ashy lips. "What can be the meaning of this?"

"I'll let Master William know what is the meaning, when I catch hold of him," was the angry rejoinder. "He must have got out on some spree with the schoolboys. But it is strange, too! He never attempted such a thing before."

"He came up to bed all right last night, sir, and went into his room," interposed Sarah, who stood in as much consternation as anybody, whilst poor Edmund looked vacantly from side to side. "The young ladies came up at the same time."

Mrs Allair drew her husband aside. "A fearful, strange dread is upon me," she uttered. "I fear he has run away."

"Run away!" repeated Mr Allair, incredulously. "What for? Where should he run to?"

She would have said "To sea," but the words refused

to come. She seized hold of a chair to save herself from falling.

"Don't distress yourself," said her husband, soothingly; "there's nothing to be alarmed at. It is not likely he should have run away, as you call it. If he has, we'll soon bring him back again, I can promise him that."

A shriek from Sarah interrupted Mr Allair. She had been gratifying her curiosity by an inspection of William's drawers. "Some of his things are gone," she called out. "Here's only three of his shirts, and not half his handkechers. He must have gone off somewhere, on the sly, I should be afeared, meaning to stop. What's that?"

It was a fall. Mrs Allair had fainted away.

The news of William's disappearance went forth to Whittermead, and the village was speedily up in arms. When back news came to be gathered and combined, scraps of fact, items of suspicion, it appeared to be only too conclusive that William *had* run away. His pressing for the sovereign the previous night appeared one very conclusive fact against him. Mr Allair did not at first admit the probability; but he was obliged to yield. Some of the schoolboys privately told him that William had "for certain" gone off to be a sailor: had gone, "for certain," to join James Carter. Mr Allair at length adopted the same view, and departed for London by the first train, in search of him.

But that was not the only surprise Whittermead was favoured with that day.

A brown, lanky, worn-looking object arrived in the afternoon at Whittermead. A contrite sort of object, with hanging head and bent eyelids. He bore some resemblance, the village thought, to Master Gruff Jones; but Master Gruff had never been seen in a shamefaced plight such as this.

Master Gruff it proved to be; and shamefaced enough. For he was come to ask grace of his father for his past rebellion, and fervently to implore never to be sent to sea again.

"So you have had enough of it!" cried the squire, his surprise a little abated, when the gentleman reached his presence.

Master Gruff, albeit getting on now to be Mr Gruff, burst into tears: long-restrained, grievous, heart-broken tears, none the less bitter for their having been for months suppressed. "Oh, father! don't send me back again!" he wailed forth. "A sailor's life on board those working vessels is worse than a dog's!"

"Highty tighty, but this is news!" exclaimed the squire. "A fine change in the weather, this! I understood you to say that in going to sea you would step into a sort of terrestrial paradise."

"Paradise!" groaned Gruff.

"You did say it. Where's the mistake, Hugh?"

"Father, it is the most awful life," wailed Hugh. "It's enough to kill a dog. There! And you are beaten black and blue besides! And instead of the ship being a beautiful, trim, clean thing, ever in apple-pie order, with her noble sails set, as you read of in Marryat's novels, or as the talk used to be in the school, and Vane boasted, she's a dirty, clumsy, unmanageable mass of ugliness, always wanting to be attended to, with no place where you can sit, and close fetid holes to sleep in, worse than your dog-kennels, and scores of rats running over you! And we are kept at labour night and day, and our naked feet and hands are cut and bruised with the work; and for weeks together we don't have a dry thread about us, for the water washes in, and soaks everything on board, clothes on and clothes off. O sir! do have pity upon me! I *can't* go back again."

Squire Jones never felt more inclined to laugh. It was precisely what he had anticipated.

"And then the language you hear; ay, and get to learn, too!" went on Mr Gruff, his sobs nearly choking him. "It's a wonder that the skies don't fall with it. And you have to eat biscuit with the maggots in it, and green beef—junk they call it—oh, it's awfully sickening. Father, I'd rather be put to sweep a crossing at home than I'd be at sea!"

"I can't believe my own ears," mocked the squire, keeping his countenance. "I have told everybody what a charming life my eldest son had entered upon; nothing that I had ever heard or read could come up to it, save fairy land, or the scenes in the 'Tales of the Genii.' How is it, I say, Hugh?"

"Don't send me back again!" besought Gruff, in his agony. "Put me into a coffin, and follow me to the grave if you like, but don't send me back again. Father, dear father! I would ten times over rather be dead and lying at peace in my grave, than live under the hardships of a sea life."

Mr Jones changed his tone to seriousness. "You chose the life, Hugh."

"I did not choose *that*—the life I found. I chose

the picture drawn by the boys and Harry Vane—the
false, pleasant aspect given to it in false books.   You
remember those two plates, father, in ' Martin Chuzzle-
wit,' of the famous city of Eden.   The beauty, the
fertility of the drawn picture, and the utter desolation
of the reality.   Well, going to sea is like those pictures :
it is an exact illustration of them ; I have thought of
them many a time in my misery, when I have been up
aloft.   We are led to look for everything that's pleasant and smooth ; but when we get afloat, we find out
the deceit, and the horrors we have entered on."

" You lead yourselves to look for smoothness, Hugh.
I told you you'd find what it seems you have found."

Gruff hung his head.   " It's true, father.   My mind
was perverted, and I would not listen to you.   Forgive
me the past, and let me stay on land.   You will not
force me to go again ?"

" Well, I don't know," said the squire, keeping up
the joke.   " Perhaps another voyage would prove better, more agreeable to you than the last has been ?"

Down went Gruff on his knees, and sobbed out his
prayer, more terrified than before.

" I should never come back again alive.   I should
die of the hardships.   Father, don't send me !"

" Will you turn rebellious again, Hugh, if I forgive
you now !"

" Never.   This has cured me, father."

" Very well.   I am glad it has.   There's nothing like
self-cure.   Get up.   Which of the two do you think
now knew best, young sir—you or I ?"

Gruff rose from his knees humble and thankful.   His
contrition was genuine, for so had been his hardships.

" Another of you is off to-day, I hear," remarked the squire—" William Allair."

" Not off to sea!" returned Gruff.

" It is supposed so. He has disappeared, nobody knows whither, taking some shirts with him. Went away in the night. He had the sea fever upon him, so there's little doubt that he is off to it."

" My goodness!" exclaimed Gruff, rubbing his tearful face. " Run away to sea! I *am* sorry for him. Poor Allair! he little thinks what it is."

" A pity but you had come home a day sooner. It might have stopped him."

" I don't know," mused Hugh, casting his thoughts back to *his* fever. " When you are regularly in for it, all the talking in the world doesn't stop you. You don't believe it, and don't listen to it."

" The only thing would be, then, to drive back the fever in its onset, not to suffer it to take hold of you," said the squire.

" Ah! if we could!—if we did but know!" lamented Gruff.

" *Could!*" returned the squire. " What do you mean by that? A right-minded lad, anxious to do his duty, does not say ' If I could.' He says ' I will.' Don't forget that, Master Hugh."

Pray don't you forget it, either, boys.

CHAPTER XIII.

BUT meanwhile where was William Allair? Speeding fast to that delightful Eden of his imagination, the sea.

He reached Liverpool unmolested, unpursued. Mr Allair, you see, was on a false scent: he had gone to London. William's object was to engage himself on board some vessel, any that was about to start, as a working sailor: he could not expect to go in a higher capacity at present. Difficulties, however, lay in his path. He had no registered ticket, no discharge, no outfit. It was his fortune, however, to fall in with people who taught him how to overcome these little obstacles: certain men called crimps, who infest seaport towns, and are ever on the look-out for victims, young men green as William Allair, green as you would be, my dear boy, were you to run blindfold into their friendly hands. They assumed the protectorship of William, and things went on swimmingly and smoothly. A ship was instantly found for him, one about to depart at once—the "Prosperous," an American vessel, hailing from New York. He bound himself to work on board her for three years, as an "apprentice," and a small outfit was provided; how very small and short, William never knew until he was at sea; the clothes he had gone down in, and the contents of his pockets, including the valuable gold watch which had been a legacy from his grandfather, being left on shore in compensation. That gold watch was worth forty pounds. He rather rebelled at the binding himself for three years; but was assured that it was the only way in which he could get to sea, and that at the end of the three years he would be promoted to the place of second mate, with immense wages. William believed his friends.

The vessel was a trader, of four hundred tons burthen, having the usual complement of men on board, all of whom were Americans, save a boy who joined when William did. The captain's name was Janns; he was of Dutch extraction, but had himself been born in the States. He was not a prepossessing man in features; truth to say, William did not like the look of him at all; but he strove to admire him as a bluff sea-captain.

There was one thing, however, that did strike on his heart with somewhat of a chill. Whenever William had thought of a ship—and it had been pretty frequently, as you know—the picture that rose up in his imagination was of a trim, elegantly-built vessel, her white sails set, and her colours waving, gliding majestically over a wide expanse of transparent waters, deep and beautiful in colour as a painter's ultramarine. Just the ship, in fact, that you see exposed for sale under a glass case, or in the paintings of some of the first masters. Gruff Jones, you may remember, had cherished the same ideas. But what did William see when he first reached Liverpool? It was a dull, rainy day; so that may have made the aspect of things worse; but he saw a heap of dirty, ugly, black-looking vessels huddled together,—a heterogeneous mass of sides, decks, spars, masts, ropes, pitch, tar, dirt, and confusion, all floating in

the muddy, turbid, yellowish-tinted water of the docks.
The sight struck coldly and oddly upon William, leaving
its natural impression.   He was not like Harry Vane.
The latter's heart yearned to a ship, no matter how unfa-
vourably viewed; William's heart already recoiled from
them, as they looked there; though he would not have
admitted the fact for the world, even to himself. "But
this will soon be changed," reasoned William.   "Let
us get a day's sail, or so, from port; leave this thick,
unpleasant-looking water behind; and give the fair ship
range on her pure native element.   That will be the
time o' day!"

The "Prosperous" was ready for sea when William
joined her. She was about returning to New York, and
it was expected would thence be sent to California—
at that time far from being deemed a desirable country
to visit. What a scene it was to William when the
vessel made preparations for getting under weigh!
Hurrying, screaming, shouting, swearing! Innumerable orders were given.   Some to him: orders which
he could not obey, simply from being at a loss to know
what was meant, and *how* he was to execute them.
Many a hard word was given him, and harder blow;
pushed hither, knocked thither; contemptuously thrust
aside, and called a lazy, sneaking land-lubber! Yards
had to be braced, sails loosed, the craft around cleared.
It appeared a maze of confusion, and William was in a
maze with it.   But the start was effected at last; the
moorings were loosened, the docks and the river were
left behind, the ship commenced her course on the sea,
rolling from side to side with the ground swell: and
William Allair was fairly launched on his perilous

voyage, and had bid adieu to England and to ease and happiness for ever.

Had William Allair wished to be treated to the ills of a sailor's life in their worst bearings, he could not have fixed upon a better ship than this identical one, the "Prosperous." Life on board her was not a favourable specimen of the American service. Hardships are found in their ships, as they are in ours.

And, as the days passed on, he became slowly but surely aware how widely different was the reality from the fabled romance he had conjured up. And then came repentance: that terrible, unavailing repentance, which saddens the brain, and turns the heart to sickness. What a life was his? How could he so madly, so blindly, have rushed upon it? He, who had not known what it was to soil his hands, who had never so much as cleaned the boots he walked in, or brushed the clothes he wore, had now to pass his days in toil that was totally unfitted for him. He, who had often said to Harry Vane that a sailor's must be a deliciously lazy life, who had laughed in derision when told the contrary, had now to find that a sailor's work is never done. From the rising of the sun to its going down, it was toil, toil, toil; added to which, there were the midnight watches, and broken rest.

Thousands like William Allair have fallen, and are falling, into the same error. "What can there be to do at sea?" they cry. If you, my inexperienced boys, feel inclined to stand upon the dispute, and make the same inquiry, take what I now tell you as an answer. The hardest, the most laborious life you can possibly fix upon, I may say the most *cruel* life, is that of a sailor's on board these merchant ships; and it is, of all others, the most comfortless. It is of no use to go into details of the labour; you would find the description tedious, and not understand at last; but rely upon it, it has broken many and many a spirit, many a heart, many a life. Gruff Jones's expression, "It is a worse life than a dog's," was not an inapt one.

No unhappy criminal at the galleys labours half so hard in his chains as did William Allair, now he was a common seaman: neither are the transports kept under more strict discipline than was he. The forecastle where he lived, in common with some dozen or fifteen others, was a dark, damp, wretched hole, so full of chests and lumber of some sort or other, that there was no room to sit or move in it. The everlasting salt junk was their food: at home he would have gone without meat for a month, rather than have touched it. The mode of taking their meals reminded him of Mr Jenniker's pigs taking theirs. A large, hard, red lump of this junk was put in a small tub in the forecastle, and each man, with his own sheath knife, cut off what he wanted. It was eaten with equally hard, unpalatable biscuit. This was the living; it was rarely varied; and the drink was water. Night and morning they had a tin jug full of tea. It was made in a furnace, some treacle stirred into it with a rolling-pin, and served out to them, tea-leaves and all. William would let his leaves settle to the bottom, but most of the sailors swallowed them with the tea. The "Prosperous" was a temperance ship, as it is called; consequently there was no grog. The captain took enough, though, for his own share.

William was not alive at first to the full ills of his position. He never thought that the incessant work was to last; he supposed it to be but what was necessary upon getting out to sea. He lay in his berth, suffering agonies from sea-sickness; too ill to pay attention to the coarse fare eaten around him: but he did gaze upon the wretched place, with its inexpressibly close, nauseous smell, that was henceforth to be his home; he gazed upon the rude, hardened crew, with whom he must fraternize. He, the refined William Allair, so unfitted, both by nature and education, to be forced into the rough companionship of such! He would henceforth have many bitter pills to swallow, but none that would be felt more annoyingly than this.

Bitter pills indeed! and in his obstinate ignorance he had honoured the articles that were to bind him to his father by the same epithet. He would recall the expression now, could he exchange his present life for the one he had then rejected.

And the time went on; and with the exception of one short note, written to his mother, Whittermead heard nothing of him, any more than it had of Dick Jenniker.

It would be nearly an impossible task to describe the sensations of Mrs Allair in the first few days following his departure: quite impossible for you fully to understand them. When convinced that he was actually *gone;* when Mr Allair returned at length from London bringing no tidings of him; then her hopes turned to letters, to receiving news from him by means of writing. But to say her "hopes" turned to that, is an expression denoting most imperfectly the state of her mind and heart. Fevered in brain, fevered in body, her nights and days were passed in one long, miserable yearning. Ten times a day would she walk to the post-office, in the fond and foolish delusion that the postman, by some unusual oversight, had forgotten to leave the letter at her house. "Is there any letter for me? Is there any letter for me?" was the burthen of her cry. And the old postmistress who dealt out the letters would silently shake her head in sympathy at the sad voice, the sadder face, and whisper a faint hope that there might be one on the morrow. People began to say, that unless news came, it would kill Mrs Allair.

At length news did come, in the shape of a letter from William himself. It was written in Liverpool, but not posted until he had sailed some days: William's "friends" took care of that. It told her little more than that he was alive and well, and about to embark on the life he had so longed for—the sea. It did not give a clue to the precise ship he had embarked in, or for what particular port he was bound; but he promised to write all these details the instant they made it. And he begged her and his father to pardon the step he had taken, to wish him good luck in his venture, and to look forward to their next joyful meeting.

Alas! even at the very hour that Mrs Allair was reading that most unsatisfactory note, William's repentance was setting in.

CHAPTER XIV.

A TASTE OF THE SEA.

THE stay of the ship "Prosperous" in New York was limited. It may be asked by many, why William Allair did not make a second run and quit the ship, as he found himself so uncomfortable upon it. Whether he would have attempted the step, I am unable to say; but at any rate he had no opportunity given him, being by far too closely watched. Possibly the captain doubted whether such might not be his intention; for he never allowed him to go on shore but once, and then it was under convoy of the mate. From this port William wrote home more fully, stating where he was, and that they were bound to the coast of California round Cape Horn. Not a word was there in his letter of having realized the pleasure he had so confidently counted on; neither was there mention of his bitter disappointment, or of his cruelly hard life; but there was a vein of sadness running through it, which told too surely its own tale, and the unhappiness of him who wrote it. So, all the tidings conveyed to his anxious relatives, to his mother, were, that he was in the severe trading service, bound upon the hardest known voyage, and that he was unhappy in body and in mind.

The "Prosperous" commenced her voyage to California from New York, passing by Cape Horn. Ah!

William had it now. If he had found the passage from
England to America bad, what did he think of this,
for a change? He wondered whether he could live
through its ills. But let us get on at present, and you
shall hear a little about it on the homeward voyage.
In about five months they arrived at their destination,
and anchored at Santa Barbara. After discharging her
cargo, the " Prosperous " was to take in another, consisting chiefly of hides ; to do which, the captain said
would occupy them full two years from the time of
arrival.

Neither is there leisure to give to the time spent off
California, whether at Santa Barbara, Monterey, San
Pedro, San Diego, or San Francisco, all of which bays,
or ports, the ship was located in by turns. But, no
matter where they were, the work was always hard,
though it varied from the monotonous labour at sea.
The landing of the cargo was sharp work, very sharp
for William Allair, especially the rolling of the weighty
casks up the hilly beach. Their whole exerted strength
scarcely prevented the barrels rolling back upon them :
their naked feet were constantly bleeding ; bruised,
and cut with the rough stones. The cargo landed,
they were employed in getting off hides from the shore
to the ship. Who that had known William Allair in
England could recognise him now? Dressed in the
roughest, lowest, meanest attire, his feet bare, his head
covered with hides—the usual mode of carrying them !
He had shrunk from a cut finger at home, delicately
wrapped up in a piece of linen rag : he had to bear
the far sharper pain of his bleeding feet. There was
no wrapping up for them ; cuts and wounds were left

undressed and exposed to the rough beach, to be cut again.

You may be puzzled to know, boys, why he did not wear shoes. It is a common practice for the working sailor to go barefoot, and it was not possible to do otherwise at that time on the Mexican coast. Shoes were not, or scarcely to be, procured there : and the beach-work, combined with the constant wetting from the surf, would have worn out a pair almost in a day.

The hides had to be cured after being collected ; or, to speak more intelligibly, to be converted into leather. This process was long, difficult, and disagreeable ; the putrid flesh, sticking to the hides in places, oppressed the men with sickening nausea, and rendered William, more delicately reared than they, frequently ill. But ill or well, he must never cease from labour. I cannot tell you whether the same long and troublesome process has to be pursued now by the crews of the vessels going to California for hides ; but I can tell you that it was the case at the time of which I am writing. In addition to this labour, the ship had to be tended and worked just as though they were at sea. The winds on the Californian coast are exceedingly violent, especially those blowing from the south-east. Often they would have to put out to sea, and remain out for days together, encountering all the danger and hardship of a storm. So sudden would be the approach of these squalls, that all hands must work away for their lives, and get the vessel from the coast ; otherwise she would have been driven on shore, and dashed to pieces. And the curing of these fragrant hides had to be pursued all the same ; for the process, once begun, must be

continued without interruption, if they would preserve
their hides and their leather.

A vastly agreeable life, was it not? Perhaps some
of you would like to try it?

But, to linger on the Mexican coast, would for us be
neither profitable nor pleasant, and I have promised
you some account of the return.

It was in the month of May, 1848—for you remember
we are not writing of very late years—that the "Prosperous" commenced her homeward voyage, after a stay
of considerably more than two years on the Californian
coast, and nearly three since William Allair's departure
from home.

Three years! Three years of hardship, toil, and
privation! without a word of love or hope from the
old house at home! Whether his friends wrote to him
or not, he did not know. In the letter William had
written from New York, he had been able to give no
definite address: and so irregular was the postage
system at that time in California, that, had they sent a
dozen letters, the chances were he never would have
received one.

The "Prosperous" was returning direct to New York,
where William would receive his wages, and whence
his intention was to proceed immediately to England.
Two of the crew were left behind at San Diego: the
hard labour, with the incessant exposure on the coast,
had wrought their effects: and when the ship was ready
to sail, they were so ill that Captain Janns would not
bring them away. Earnestly they implored not to be
left on that inhospitable, half savage shore; but the
captain coarsely answered, with an oath, that sick men

were not wanted on board ship. In point of fact, this
is true. If a sailor falls sick on board, he must get
well as he best can ; there is nobody to nurse him. So
the men were left; which rendered the vessel two
hands short.

As they neared Cape Horn, the weather became fear-
fully hard. They expected to pass it in July, the very
worst month of all the twelve in that region of perpetual winter. By the latter end of June, they had
come up with what the experienced sailors called Cape
weather. Often, after their long, cheerless watch on
deck, the men had scarcely descended to the forecastle,
when " All hands ahoy!" would send them back flying:
sails must be taken in with double-quick speed, to wear
through the squall that was coming. On, would come
the blast ; long before they were ready for it ; sleet,
snow, rain, and wind. Such wind! Never on shore let
us talk again of the wind taking our breath away! The
heavily laden ship would be thrown nearly on her beam
ends, her timbers cracking, her top-gallant masts bending, the foam dashing over her bows, as she careered
madly through the storm. The hands climbed aloft :
what though the hail cut their faces, and nearly blinded
them, as it drove horizontally across the ocean, and the
violent wind impeded almost entirely their movements !
—still they must work the ship. It was no child's
play. The sails were as hard as boards, but they must
be hauled and furled, and the men were wet through
as they stood upon the yards; their hands, already
stiffened and numbed, had to be beaten fiercely on the
sails to prevent the fingers freezing. Not so quickly
could they get through the business as they might

have done under better auspices; it was impossible to go along quickly, with the shrouds and rigging iced over; also, they were short of hands. An hour, an hour and a half, two hours would pass, ere the task was done: and the half-frozen, hard-worked crew would descend from its completion, to find the hour had just struck for their watch on deck to be resumed.

It was on one of these days that the English lad, who had joined the ship at Liverpool at the same time as William Allair, got into trouble with the captain. His name was Robert Stone: commonly known on board as "Bob." Captain Janns was not of choice language at any time, but in moments of anger it became—well, what would not look orthodox upon paper. Showered down upon the unhappy Bob, it was not orthodox either, at least to his thinking, for he believed he was undeserving of it: and fatigued and worn out with his hard work, he answered insolently. One word led to another on both sides; and the captain, unused to have his harshest mandate reflected on, flew into a foaming passion, and ordered Bob to be seized up. The whole crew was summoned to witness the spectacle. Stone was made fast to the shrouds, his back bared; and the captain himself undertook the office of castigator.

The rope whirled in the air, and descended —
Once!

"Oh, spare me! spare me!" shrieked Bob, leaping up with the pain.

Twice! "I'll spare you," retorted the captain, "when I have brought you to your senses! I'll teach you what it is to brave me."

Thrice! four times! ever so many times; until the

unhappy culprit fainted. And William Allair, sick with horror, thought he should have fainted too. It was a widely different exhibition, this, from the milder one bestowed upon Richard Jenniker in the old school-room.

Half an hour elapsed. The larboard watch were keeping their watch on deck. Bob Stone belonged to this watch; but it may be thought by you inexperienced land boys that he was at any rate let off work for that day. No such thing. Bob's back had been treated to a wash of salt and water, and Bob himself was at his post on deck. Bob had not opened his lips since; and a sullen expression of pain pervaded his countenance. A gloomy silence reigned in the ship. The captain paced the deck, zigzag fashion, for the cargo stowed there left little room for walking; the mate stood to windward, looking at the appearance of the weather; when a sudden command, "Lay aloft there and unfurl the sails," was heard.

The men of the larboard watch prepared to man the rigging. Bob Stone alone went slowly. By those looking on, it may have been thought he went unwillingly: but that unfortunate back of his may have been alone in fault.

"Do you want another flogging?" roared the captain, as he sprang towards him, with an oath. "What are you loitering for, you skulking land-lubber?"

He dragged himself up painfully: that was evident; and bore a hand with the rest. The captain recommenced his zigzag step, and the mate stretched out his hand for the night glass: he did not much like appearances out to windward.

"What's that?" cried he.

It was a sudden splash in the water: just as if a heavy weight had dropped, dash, into it. The captain and mate hurried to the vessel's side.

"A man overboard! A man overboard!" rose up the cry, echoing from one end of the ship to the other. Down came the men from the yards, like cats, eager to get out the quarter boat, before the order could be spoken.

One of the men had dropped from the yards aloft. Which of them? The larboard watch looked at one another: the captain looked at them collectively. The missing one was Bob Stone.

The boat was got off, and rowed towards the spot; but the ill-fated Bob was never seen again. In vain they strained their eyes around; no trace could be discerned of him, and the boat put back again.

"That makes a third hand gone!" was the comment of the sailors, one to another. "How shall we be able to wear the ship round the Cape?"

If William Allair had felt sick at the flogging, how did he feel now? An inward prayer went up to God, that the unhappy lad might have slipped unwittingly from the yards; and not have thrown himself off, in his shame and unhappiness.

Ere the boat had been made fast again, night was closing in; *their* night. At that period of the year, round Cape Horn, the sun, on favourable days, rises at nine and sets at three: but it is not often they can get to see the sun at all. A dismal scene, it was, that lonesome ship and her isolated crew. Many hundred miles away from available land: exposed to all the incle-

mencies of a Cape winter; living almost in a perpetual
night; in danger of being drifted down by floating
masses of ice, tokens of which they had already begun
to see; the dreadful hardships of their life and position cannot well be exaggerated. And now the visit
of Death! No wonder that the men felt their spirits
sinking!

The night set in heavily. Rain, sleet, and hail came
down upon them; and the wind howled with an ominous sound. The thermometer had fallen greatly since
the morning, which called forth the mate's opinion that
they must be near large ice islands. Mrs Allair had
used to complain if William got his feet wet, or was out
in the rain so as to damp his jacket. It was a mercy,
William thought, that she did not see what he was
exposed to now. It may be said that the men lived in
water. All the clothing they possessed (and very short
and scant it was!) was perpetually wet: there were no
means of drying it. Did the sun peep lazily out, their
things would be hung up, but they did not dry. After
a severe watch of four hours, they would take their
clothes off in the forecastle, wring the water from
them, and put on the change from which the water had
been in a like manner previously wrung. But the discomfort of the wet clothes was nothing, compared to
that of the boots—thick boots being indispensable to a
Cape Horn attire. Always saturated with wet were
they, rendering the feet miserably cold. You may get
your feet warm in bed, young gentlemen; but you are
not rounding Cape Horn, in a Cape winter. The berths
on board the "Prosperous" were as wet as the men,
for they could only get into them in their wet clothing.

Perhaps you are indulged with a fire in your bed-chamber, when there is a little frost on the ground? Some boys get it, who are coddled up, not brought up. They should try William Allair's life for a day, just by way of change. His face and hands were often cut with the large, sharp hailstones; and these same hands, their wounds exposed, must hold on by the hulls and spars, a mass of ice, hauling and pulling the stiffened sails, and taking knots with the running rigging, the ropes so hard that there was no bending them. The men's clothes froze upon them. It was with some difficulty they could prevent their bodies freezing also. There was no comfort for them, no ease, no semblance of either: and their snatches of sleep in their damp berths would be all too frequently interrupted with the arousing cry,—"All hands ahoy!"

But, to go back to this night. Its long, tedious eighteen hours wore away; and when the dawn broke, they found the mate's opinion, that they were coming to the ice, to be correct. On this day the sun was out, and it shone brightly. About twelve o'clock they came in view of an iceberg. It was the most beautiful sight conceivable: the strangest and finest picture possible to be imagined. No painting has ever done justice to an iceberg, neither can any description: an island of ice, shaped like a mountain, its height tapered off into transparent pinnacles, and its general colour azure, shading imperceptibly into the pure white of the pinnacles, whose glittering tops were brilliant in the sun, the waves rising white and foaming at its base. A wondrously grand object was it, as it moved through the clear, blue waters with slow and stately action.

Occasionally it was heard to crack with a noise like thunder, and portions of it dropped away into the sea below, causing the waves to dash aloft and fall again, like so many cascades of silver.

As the ship bore cautiously on her course, innumerable ice islands appeared, some large, some small; and also large tracts, or fields, of floating ice, causing their progress to be exceedingly difficult and dangerous. It was next to impossible to steer the ship clear of them. The captain and crew were quite alive to their peril; they were in constant apprehension that one or other of these masses of ice would drift against the ship and stave her in, in which case nothing could have saved them. "The boats?" suggests some green little boy. How would you steer a boat amidst those floating mounds of ice? And, even if the boats could live, you would be frozen to death in a few hours, off Cape Horn.

On the second day of their reaching these fields of ice, it began to blow a gale when the sun went down. Or it may be better to say, when daylight declined; for the sun had been visible but for a few minutes, and then it looked like a copper-coloured ball. The ship was tossed hither and thither, the hail and sleet whistled around them, and, to add to the dangers of their situation, a dense fog came on. What an anxious night were they about to pass! Eighteen hours of darkness, with a fog so thick that nothing could be discerned at a few yards' distance, the ship in momentary danger of being stove in by some floating mass of ice, or of going to pieces on an ice island! The captain ordered the ship to be hove-to, and then sent for all hands aft. He told them that they were in imminent peril, and that not a soul must quit the deck that night. The men had their respective stations assigned them, whence they would keep as sharp a look-out as the fog and darkness permitted, feeling that ere the dawn of another day, the ship and all that she contained might have disappeared beneath the waters. They went, silent and anxious, each man to his post. Slowly the night dragged its course along, the various notices that ice was near, from one watch or other, forming the only break to its painful monotony. It was blowing frightfully from the east, and the hail and snow beat sharply against the men. The captain was mostly on deck; if he retired to his cabin for a few minutes, the mate took the command.

At daybreak, nine in the morning, some of the men went below for breakfast, nearly dropping with fatigue and anxiety, and stiff with the ice on their clothes. No refreshment had been given them during the long suspense of that ever-to-be-remembered night; not a taste of anything. The captain and mate had partaken of some in the cabin more than once, but nothing had been offered to the worn-out men. Some snatches of sleep were obtained by them in turn during the daylight; and with three o'clock P.M. again came the dark, and the fatigue and anxiety of the previous night had once more to be endured.

This continued for some days; the fog and the gales, coupled with the dangerous ice, compelling the ship to be still hove-to. William Allair's station had been, part of the time, the very worst on the ship; it was upon the forecastle, a place excessively exposed to the wind and weather. Anxiety, remorse, despair, and fear—

the incessant fear that each hour would be his last—
in conjunction with the toil and hardships of his lot,
were working their effects upon him, rendering him
ill in body as he had long been in mind. A slow fever
attacked him, ripening into a remittent one as the days
went on.

He became very ill with it. But, ill as he was, he
might not quit his work, for it would have rendered
another hand to be counted short in the already badly-
manned ship. Moments of delirium passed across his
brain when lying between the watches in his damp
berth in the wretched forecastle, and he would vainly
endeavour to close his eyes in sleep. Pictures would
arise of his happy home, the home he had so recklessly
and blindly given up; a remembrance of the case he
had enjoyed, the serenity of the line of life chalked out
for him, contrasting bitterly with his present toil and
sufferings. Even the old office, then so despised and
hated, was now regarded as a very haven of calmness
and rest. Visions of his dear mother were of frequent
occurrence. In that state, half sleep, half delirium,
induced by fever, he would fancy he saw her. Sometimes she was ill and grieving after him, sometimes she
would look well and happy as of yore; but always was
she yearning for and anticipating the period of his return. Once he fancied—it was but a repetition of his
waking thoughts, his unceasing longings—that he was
back again; his mother all joy; his father, though at
first chiding, all forgiveness; his sisters clinging round
him; his poor brother wild with glee. And what
seemed his own sensations? Why, they might be
compared to those of one who has quitted misery for

Elysium. His toils and troubles at sea were over, and he was with his family, never, never to leave them, never to go near the hated sea again. But he was not quit of the sea yet.

"Eight bells there, below—do you hear?" broke violently his dream; and starting up, he rushed on deck with his shipmates. A day and a night he did lie by; there was no help for it. A miserable place, though, was that forecastle to be in! The water dripped down on all sides of it, lumber and wet clothes filled up its confined space; while the air was unpleasantly fetid and pernicious, chiefly from its being kept closely shut up. As to the living? Why, sick or well, there was the salt junk tub. His head was racked with pain; his limbs were now shivering with ague, now burning with fever; his tongue and throat were parched. How he would have been waited and tended on at home! But here there was no consolation; there were none to help him!

But we will not follow him in his illness, or the ship through the *weeks* that they tried in vain to double Cape Horn. William Allair had deliberately brought all this discomfort upon himself. One vague hope—it seemed too far off to be anything but vague in their present peril—did buoy up his sinking heart : the hope that it would all be as he had seen it in his feverish dream.

CHAPTER XV.

THE weary weeks wore away, and the ship progressed.
A happy day on board was that, when they left the
Cape behind them. They had finer weather after passing it, and a change for the better became not a hope,
but a certainty. Each day the sun began to get higher,
though the ice on the ship did not yet thaw; whilst
every night sank some constellation in the south, and
raised a more familiar one in the northern horizon.
When William had first seen the groups of stars he had
been accustomed to live under, disappear and give place
to strange ones, the Magellan clouds, the Southern
Cross, a sharp undefined feeling of dread would shoot
across him; it seemed as if he was going into an unknown world.

And now the good ship went on gallantly, bearing
a press of sail. They had got into open water and open
weather, as the sailors called it. Hey for home!
William's heart leaped to every knot she made; and
he almost dared to whisper to himself that God had
seen how terrible had been his punishment, and would
in mercy forgive him and send him safely home again.

Fair and gently! Stop a bit. This favourable change
was not to last to the end. After some prolongation
of it, which had got them well forward, the weather one
morning altered. Squalls of wind and rain came on,

which soon increased to half a gale, and the look-out —to use the words of the mate—was downright ugly. The captain ordered the courses to be reefed and furled, the sails secured, and all other precautions taken against the storm that was threatening.

A dark, heavy night set in. The gale increased, the captain remained on deck, and the ship laboured much, the boiling waves rushing over her bows and flinging their foam aloft. Now she rose on the heaving waves, now she buried her black shrouds in the deep, her tall masts rising and sinking, looking—had there been any distant spectators—like a thing supernatural amidst the surrounding gloom. Suddenly she plunged wildly forward, and encountered a heavy sea, which threw her on her beam ends. There was a sharp, affrighted cry, and one of the sailors came forward, terror on his countenance. The vessel had shipped a quantity of water.

The mate rushed to the hold. It was even as the man said. The ship had sprung a leak. A short while, and the water rose up to five feet.

All hands were set to work at the pumps; and after some hours' labour, the quantity was considerably decreased. The leak was found, and the carpenter set about repairing it. But the gale increased. By the morning it was blowing awfully. The captain's face wore a look of anxiety, while the mate seemed to be gifted with ubiquity, so many parts of the ship was he seen in, almost at the same moment.

The wind abated a little with the broad daylight; but when the sun went down, the storm came on again with terrific violence. Another leak was sprung; either the former had re-opened, or the fresh one was close to it, and the water rushed in impetuously. Everything was done that could be, in their unhappy situation. The pumps were worked incessantly, the captain strove to give his orders cheerfully : whatever his faults of temper, he was a thorough seaman, and the men obeyed him. They worked, but not with a will ; one dark thought weighed down their spirits—that they might, before morning, be in another world. Oh, what an awful time it was ! we, who have lived all our lives on shore, can form no idea of it. The night pitchy dark ; the wind howling and shrieking in gusts that seemed to be almost unearthly ; the crashing of the timbers as the masts rent and toppled ; the devoted ship, huge and shadowy in the night's gloom, crying and groaning as she was tossed about with the blast ; the waves rushing mountains high, foaming and hissing, beating over and against the ship, buffeting those who were in her. The ill-fated men plyed away at the pumps, their spirits and their bodies sinking, but conscious that it was their one only chance for life. Every moment threatened to dash the ship in pieces. Her mizen-mast and rudder had been carried away, and her decks swept. Two of the seamen, poor fellows, were already gone. Worn out with fatigue, numbed with the cold, bruised and battered by the tempest, they had been washed away, not having the strength to hold on, while performing some necessary duty.

And was it for this that William Allair had quitted his sheltering home? to endure years of never-ceasing hardship, and at last to perish far away, amidst the horrors of that night?

It was now a matter of certainty that the ship was

K

gradually sinking, and they must meet their fate with what calmness and resignation they could. Another soul, the second mate, was washed overboard. Nothing more could be done; the pumps were abandoned in despair; three of the crew climbed up to the main rigging, deeming that a few minutes more of life would be left to them there than if they remained below.

With the morning, the violence of the storm had worn itself out, and the sea was, comparatively speaking, calm. The captain announced to the mate that he had resolved to make one trial for their lives, by trusting themselves to the jolly boat, which, strange to say, had not been swept away.

The mate shook his head. He did not think it possible the boat could live, even if they could succeed in launching it and getting safely into it.

"It is worth the trial," argued the captain. "To remain in the ship is certain destruction. In a few hours her masts will be under water. I am aware that death is almost as certain, and may, perhaps, be quicker in the boat; still there is a chance. Life is sweet to us all."

"Oh, try it, sir!" uttered William, clasping his hands in supplication. "If there be but the faintest glimmering of hope, let us try it, rather than die here!"

The captain turned sharply upon him. But common peril has a wonderful tendency to equalize men; and the breach of discipline passed unreproved.

The sailors were called from the rigging, where they had climbed; but they did not answer, and remained immovable. They had been frozen to death amidst the horrors of that fatal night.

With immense difficulty the boat was launched, another life having been lost in the process. The captain lowered himself into it last. "God alone," said he, "can save and help us now."

And God did help them, and carried them in safety away from that wreck, through the tempestuous sea, in the direction they wished to go. Ere they were out of sight of the ship, the water had nearly engulfed her, the feet of the dead men, as they dangled from the rigging, being just immerged in it.

Four days passed away, and that frail boat and its suffering crew were still at the mercy of the waters. The weather, meantime, had become beautifully serene and mild, and there was a favourable breeze to fill their bit of canvas, that they were fain to call a sail. This was the fifth day that they had been drifting on that desolate sea; no land, no sail in view to cheer their drooping spirits; no eye conscious of their need of help, save ONE. Their stock of sustenance, consisting of biscuit and water, was running low, although they had been, from the first, on the shortest allowance, the captain pointing out the necessity of the food being eked out. The nights were raw and cold, exposed, as they were, in the open boat; but as they drew nearer to the equator, towards which, happily to say, the wind continued to drift them, the temperature grew milder.

They suffered greatly from thirst, a very small quantity of water being doled out each morning. If a shower of rain fell, they spread handkerchiefs—all they had—to catch it; and when they were thoroughly wet, they wrung the rain out, and drank it. This afforded some relief. The captain's character appeared to be

entirely changed since the commencement of their sufferings ; but nothing subdues a man like the fear of
approaching death. There was a Prayer Book in the
boat ; it had belonged to poor Bob Stone, and the
captain had brought it with him from the ship. Each
day he read prayers to the men, never omitting the service to be used in peril at sea. The men bared their
heads, and listened reverently. Hardened as they were,
reprobate as they had been, there was not one but sup-
plicated fervently for forgiveness, whether it should be
their fate to live or die.

But now, for two successive days and nights, they
had no rain ; their allowance of water was less, and the
most intolerable thirst prevailed. Another day, and
the pangs of famine were added to those of thirst, their
biscuit being exhausted. The carpenter and one of the
other men yielded to the temptation of drinking the sea
water, although cautioned against it by the rest, who
declared they would endure any amount of suffering
rather than attempt it. It produced a widely different
effect upon the two. The carpenter seemed renovated
and refreshed by it, suffering no evil consequences ;
while the other, in a short space of time, died in deli-
rious agony.

And, next, the captain began to sink. Of all those
in the boat, the one who might be supposed least calculated to battle with the hardships of their situation was
William Allair. Yet he appeared to bear up manfully ;
while the captain, a strong man and hearty, was slowly
resigning his life. It was a calm, peaceful evening, that
on which he died. The sun was drawing towards the
west, and its beams fell aslant upon his pallid features.

He knew he should not see it rise on the morrow. With a feeble farewell to the men, he leaned his head upon William's shoulder, next to whom he sat, and never moved again. William heard him softly praying. Ah, my boys, what a mercy it is that we have a God, a Saviour to fly to, in our extremity of need! When the sun rose in the morning they were consigning his body to the deep ; the mate, though himself scarcely able to speak, reading over him the service for the burial of the dead at sea. I hope his spirit was happy!

A fearful thought began to pervade the boat. You may guess what it was, if you are familiar with accounts of this kind of suffering. The pains of hunger are grievous to be borne, the love of life is strong, and ——; but they drove away the horrible thought for the present.

Again returned the dawn of day, and there was no relief. About mid-day another died. William Allair, the only good scholar left in the boat—in fact, the only scholar of any account who had been in it, or in the ship—feebly read the prayers over him as they threw him into the sea. The mate was too far gone to attempt it.

And now the dreadful thought, above alluded to, passed into words. William Allair raised his voice against it; the mate also, who collected strength to speak. William told them that where the unnatural food had been resorted to, those partaking of it had become raving mad, and so died.

Before the discussion ended, the night closed in, and they tacitly agreed to leave its decision until the morning. When that morning came, the mate was dead, and William Allair was in a feverish stupor. The men were desperate now, and bruited a question amongst themselves: should they draw lots, or should they kill him—William?

But what is that object in the distance? One of the sailors spies it out. *A sail!* And making towards them! Oh, surely it cannot be! And yet—IT IS! God had remembered them at last.

Such was the depression and lethargy of the men, that they mostly looked at it with a stupid, unmeaning stare. But soon they burst into tears; and the carpenter, taking the book, read from it a prayer of thanksgiving in his untutored accent.

Gallantly came on the good ship. And now it neared them; and now it was abreast of them. Her captain turned away his face as he drank in at a glance the sorrow and suffering disclosed to view. The mate was in the boat, unburied; for they had been too weak, perhaps too apathetical, to be in a hurry to throw him overboard.

The hearty, rough sailors, compassionate in their help as women, descended from their ship, and tenderly bore the weak on board in their arms. By proper care and attention all were recovered. But when William Allair first awoke to the change, his confused thought was that he was in an angel's ship, sailing to the blessed port of Heaven.

CHAPTER XVI.

THE MEETING IN CALCUTTA.

THE vessel which had picked them up proved to be the barque " Texas," bound from one of the ports of Brazil to Calcutta. Here was an overwhelming disappointment to William !—he was about to be borne once more far away from his home. But there was no help for it; and he could not in gratitude quarrel with the means which had saved his life. He, with the other men saved, assisted to work the ship, she being short of hands; a fever having carried off four or five of her crew, after the " Texas" left port. But she was healthy now. The carpenter was especially welcome, their own having been one of those who had died.

As if to compensate for their previous disasters, the voyage to Calcutta was most favourable, and performed in a remarkably short time. When they reached that port, William Allair quitted the ship : he was not wanted longer. So there he was, adrift in the world in a strange land : possessing nothing ; not even a shred of clothing, save what he stood upright in. 1848 was now drawing to a close.

His whole thoughts were directed towards getting to England. And the only way open to him to accomplish that, was by working his passage over. Down he went to the river, to see if there were any craft about to sail who might require hands. Moored there was a small brig, containing some officers and men belonging (as was told to William) to a fine frigate lying at Diamond Harbour—a British man-of-war. His informant said that he heard hands were wanted for the frigate. William resolved to go on board the brig, and get himself engaged, if possible. He was extremely anxious; for he began to fear that he was again growing ill. In point of fact, he had not recovered the fever, or the hardships following upon it.

He made his way on to the brig, which was called the "Lord Hastings," and was waiting to be spoken to, when his attention was attracted to a tall, handsome young officer pacing the quarter-deck. Not for his fine figure did William regard him, not for his prepossessing looks; but because the face seemed known to him.

Where had he seen it? He could not recollect. The features were familiar; and yet not familiar. Once, as a brother officer passed and spoke, the object of William's attention smiled in reply. That smile awoke a strange thrill in his heart, for it seemed to call up remembrances of Whittermead.

"Who is that gentleman?" inquired William, of the steward's man, who was standing by.

"That? He's one of our lieutenants. Mr Vane."

The flush of awaking recollection flew to William's countenance. Could it be? "What is his Christian name?" he hastily asked.

"His Christian name? Well—let's see. Oh, it's Harry."

"Belonging to the 'Hercules?'"

"The 'Hercules,' Captain Stafford."

"This is not the 'Hercules?'"

" *This* the ' Hercules !' You are not much of a sailor, young fellow ; or else you have never heard what her tonnage is. Why, she's a seventy-gun ship! Vessels of that class can't get up here; they have to stop at Diamond Harbour. This brig is only a temporary thing that we got to bring us up the Ganges to Calcutta. You won't see many a finer man than Lieutenant Vane."

It was even so ! His dear old companion and friend, Harry Vane, stood before him. The man talked on, but William heard him not. For one brief moment he forgot his position : the tide of memory ebbed back to the past, obliterating the present ; there was the Harry Vane of their school days, and he was William Allair. He took a step forwards : pleasurable eagerness in his eyes, his hand extended, an exclamation on his lips ; but recollection returned to him in time, and he retreated again. What ! should he—a common sailor, low in rank, shabby in appearance, applying on the ship for work—should he dare to advance to the quarter-deck, and boldly offer his hand, and claim acquaintance with one of its chief officers? Back ! back, William Allair ! you deliberately chose your own station in life, and you must abide by it.

The heart bitterness rose in his throat as if it would have suffocated him. He turned away ; and, without saying a syllable to anybody, left the ship. He must find some other means of going home, or stay in India. Anything rather than join the " Hercules."

The next day, William was lying in Calcutta Hospital, with an attack of incipient brain fever. The severity of the voyage round Cape Horn, the privations, the exposure on the open sea, and now the dreadful heat

raging in Calcutta, all combined to induce it. Added to
which causes, must be classed his remorse and anxiety
of mind. The attack, in truth, was a slight one; more
to be called a threatening than a positive attack. The
remedies applied were prompt, and in a few days its
danger had passed; but it left him deplorably weak
and spiritless, and, as he believed, dying.

Oh! his had been a bitter fate! To have toiled hard,
lived hard, and now to die in an Indian hospital! Without a familiar face around him! without a possibility
of sending a farewell word to the mother he had so
rashly disobeyed and cast aside!

Yes, there was a chance. If the brig "Hastings"
had not sailed, he might send to Harry Vane. Unless
the latter's nature was strangely altered, he would not
fail to come at the summons, although it was but to see
a poor sick sailor. A sick sailor! Harry Vane would
have tramped to the end of the world to relieve one.
He would bear home William's dying messages. But
how was he to be communicated with?

Means for that seemed to rise up without searching.
In the next bed to William's lay a young man who was
frequently visited by a sailor, an Englishman. William
had been too ill to take much note of this previously;
but when the man came again, he spoke to him.

"Do you know," he feebly asked, beckoning the man
to him, as he was about to leave his friend, "whether
the brig 'Lord Hastings' has gone down the river?"

"Not yet," was the answer. "But I fancy she'll be
off by to-morrow, for they have been busy aboard her
all day, getting her into sailing trim. Our ship's a-lying
alongside of her, and I only wish we was a-doing the

like. I hate this horrid weather: it have broiled some of us pretty nigh to death since we come. I have been froze stiff at the North Pole, and thought nothing o' that, compared with this here heat."

"Will you take a note for me on board the 'Hastings?'"

" Two if you like; notes not being weighty to carry. If they was, I don't know as I could. I might be afraid of melting, perhaps."

" When are you going down ? "

" Straight on ahead now."

" Will you reach me my clothes, and get out my pencil ? There's a piece of paper, too, somewhere."

" Sharp's the word, and quick's the motion," cried the good-natured sailor, as he sought and found the articles required.

William strove to use them; but the paper clattered in his emaciated hands, and the pencil fell. " I am too weak," he sighed. " You must deliver a message instead."

" With all my heart. What is it ?"

" Ask to see Mr Vane. He is one of the lieutenants. Tell him that—that I—tell him that a sailor is lying here, and craves to see him."

" Who shall I say ? Any name ?"

" Say ——" But William would not utter his name, that it should be spoken out aloud on board the " Hastings." Harry Vane might have talked of his old companion to his brother officers. " I think I can write just a word," he said.

By the help of the sailor, who propped him up, he contrived to scrawl the words, " William Allair, Whittermead."

" Give him that," he said, folding the paper. " And tell him to come in mercy, for that I am dying."

" Avast there !" said the man, with a hearty cheer, which was cut short in the bud by remembering where he was. " Never you give way about ' dying,' or take up any such notions ! It's this gloomy place you be in —giving you sick folks the mollygrubs, and all sorts of blues. *You'll* be well enough in a week or two, com- rade. Cheer up ! I say."

The man departed, and went on board the " Lord Hastings," as he had promised. Lieutenant Vane was not there ; he had gone ashore. So he could but leave the paper and a message. " That the young man what was writ in there was a-dying up at the hospital. Leastways, he thought he was a-dying, and wanted Mr Vane to go up quick and see him."

When Harry Vane reached the hospital, it was past the hour for visitors ; but he procured admittance. William was lying then in an uneasy slumber : but, as if conscious of who was bending over him, scarcely had Harry Vane scanned his countenance, when he started up awake.

With his burning, trembling, eager hands, he seized those that were extended to him. The emotion was too much ; and, reduced and wretched as he was, he burst into tears, and sobbed like a child.

Harry Vane leaned over him. He pressed his wasted hands in his, he spoke soothing words of calmness, he held a cup of water to his lips. A little while, and William lay quiet, but exhausted. It was the Harry Vane of other days ; affectionate, cordial, impetuous ; ready to make as much of William—the friendless,

beaten-down, poor apprentice sailor—as though he had
been a royal middy.

A few whispered explanations passed between them :
it was not the time or place for lengthened ones. William's state was too weak to admit of it, and Harry
Vane had to hurry back to the brig. She was on the
point of sailing ; and he was left in command of her
down to Diamond Harbour. He had not been to
England, he said, since he first left it ; but the
" Hercules " was ordered home now.

" Have you ever heard anything of me ? Did any of
them speak of me in their letters ?"

" Often. Caroline especially. I heard all about
your going off, and have lived in hopes of dropping
across you at some lucky port or other."

" I was not like you," said William, with a bitterness
he could not disguise. " You went with the approbation of your parents, and things have prospered with
you : I left them in rebellious defiance, and—am the
wreck you see. You used to say to Gruff Jones that
an expedition entered into in disobedience would never
prosper."

" I often said it. I hold the same opinion still.
Talking of Gruff, did he not soon have enough of it ?"

" I don't know. I have heard nothing since I left.
Did he ?"

Harry Vane laughed. " I thought he would. He
was not cut out for the sea. He is a gentleman now,
lording it as the squire's heir : and rides to cover."

William sighed. " You get news, I suppose, of your
brother Fred ? How is he ?"

Harry Vane's face became somewhat clouded. " I

don't hear much of any of them, and I have not heard recently," he answered. "The 'Hercules' has gone from place to place, and we miss our letters. Fred has been in trouble, I fear."

"What sort of trouble?" questioned William.

"He has been spending too much. A fellow with nothing to do with his time, hands and brain alike idle, must get into some mischief: it's almost a thing of necessity. Fred should have embraced some profession, if only to keep him straight. But I have not heard for some time, and I hope things are right again."

"What parts of the world have you been in?" resumed William.

"In several. But if——" he looked at William's wasted countenance, and somewhat altered the words he was about to speak—"when we meet again, I'll give you details. There's no time now."

"Are you still fond of the sea?" and the question was uttered more like an exclamation.

"I am. Not but that it's a sharp sort of life. I think I could scarcely live on land. You know," he added, with a smile, "they used to tell me I was not fit to live there."

"They were right. You were constituted for a sea life: I, not—as they used to tell *me*. I would not listen to them; I thought I knew better than they did; I was bent on following out my own obstinate self-will. Heaven knows I have paid for it."

"But there has been a wide contrast in the service we have seen," rejoined Harry. "You have experienced the darkest shades of a sea life; I, the bright ones. Passionately fond as I was of the sea, I should not have relished a Cape Horn voyage after hides, in a Yankee trader."

"You are about returning to England now?"

"Immediately; and I hope we shall not be long making it. The 'Hercules' is a fast sailer."

"And to Whittermead?"

"You may be sure I shall go there the instant I can get leave, after we touch land. Satisfied as I am with the sea, it has not taken from me the longing to see home and its ties. Do you remember my careering through the place, with the blue ribbons round my hat, when my appointment arrived? What a young donkey I was!"

"Will you bear a message for me to my home?"

"Why ask the question, William? Would I could bear you with it! I wish you could be removed on board!" he continued, impulsively. "But your malady —fever—bars it."

"I sent for you to-day, that you might take a word of love home for me. The thought that I was left here to die, neglected and friendless as any poor stray dog might be, was helping to kill me. When I knew you were at Calcutta, and could convey news of me home, it eased death of half its load. Otherwise I would not have troubled or pained you by making myself known."

"William!"

"A few days ago, before this illness came on, I was on board the 'Lord Hastings,' and recognised you. I was nearly as close to you as I am now."

Harry Vane stared. "Why in the world did you not let me know it?"

"In the impulse of the moment, in the joy at meet-

ing you, I was starting forward with extended hands;
but I recalled my senses before committing myself. I
had forgotten how changed were our positions since we
last met; how I had dropped in the scale of society."

"And I should have flown with open arms to meet
you, there or elsewhere," cried Harry Vane, in excitement. "Change of position, indeed! Is that a reason
for shunning an old friend? Never, in my creed. It
never was, and it never will be. You ought not to
have gone off the brig, leaving me in ignorance that
you had been there."

"I had the wretchedest old pea-jacket on, and
patched trousers!"

"Old pea-jacket! patched trousers!" reiterated
Harry Vane. "What on earth has that to do with it?
If a fellow I cared for came to me without either,
painted down blue instead, he'd be all the more welcome. You would have been my dear past friend,
William, introduced to my brother officers as such, just
as heartily as if you had been clothed in purple and
gold. We shan't look askance at old pea-jackets in
heaven. The world never could beat any of that sort
of pride into me when I was a youngster, you know,
and I have not learnt it yet. I say, old fellow, bear
up; you are growing exhausted."

"See them at home—my father, my sisters,"
whispered William, who felt his strength sinking. "Tell
them how severe has been my punishment; that I had
not been *a day* at sea before I began to repent, to suspect how full of hardship and misery was the life I
had embraced. Tell them that from that moment to
this I have never had an hour's enjoyment, an hour's

rest from toil. I have had no peace of mind. My time has been passed in the vain yearning for home, in futile endeavours to repress the stings of repentance."

"I don't think you ought to excite yourself like this."

"And see my mother, Harry. My dear, dear mother! See her alone. Tell her, that in all the trouble I have borne since I left her, and which has gone well-nigh to madden me, I have never ceased to think of her. Tell her that the remembrance of my ungrateful conduct, in leaving her as I did, has been to me as the very core of my anguish. Tell her that until I left home I did not know how dear she was to me; and that the misery I have endured, the illness that is upon me, the death which may overtake me, I feel that I have no right to murmur at, for they are but the result of my conduct to her—a child's ingratitude working out its retribution."

"Now, I won't stop to listen to this despondency," cried Harry Vane. "I'll deliver your messages, but I shall just say the state you were in. When a fellow's sick, it's all gloom, gloom, gloom! You will get home yet, and be the happiest of the happy there, from the very contrast those days will present to these."

"Oh that it were so! that it could be so! Do you know," William continued, while the flush of fever and excitement lighted up his cheek, "there were times when I dreamt that it would? And it is this hope—if you can call any feeling so faint and vague a hope— which has sustained me, and helped me to battle with my untoward fate."

"And let it enable you still to battle with it!" rejoined Harry Vane, fervently.

L.

"Tell my mother, that if I do live to reach home, it will have been the remembrance of her that has borne me on my way; otherwise, I *must* have sunk. And tell her that if I should not live to see her, and hear her whisper my forgiveness, her name and a prayer for her happiness will be one of the last upon my lips in dying."

"I will tell her all. But bear manfully up, William, and you will one day tell her yourself. What fun we'll have, you and I, when we get once more together at Whittermead! Won't it be a joyous time! Won't we set the bells to ring! Cheer up, old boy!"

Lieutenant Vane departed, and sailed down the river the next morning in command of his brig. He was but the third lieutenant; the second, who had come up in charge of her, had fallen ill; hence it devolved upon him.

And William was left in the hospital.

CHAPTER XVII.

WILLIAM ALLAIR slowly recovered. In the hospital, a few beds removed from his own, a sick soldier had been lying. This man, who grew convalescent before William, used to come to William's bed, sit on it, and talk to him. His name was Alfred Langly, an Englishman, of liberal education. An intimacy ensued between them. Both were strangers in the strange land, both were sick in the strange hospital, both had been reared to occupy a better position in life. For the first time since he left Whittermead, William confided who he was to this young man, the trials he had undergone, and his earnest desire to reach home, though without knowing now how he should get there. To go as a working sailor could not be thought of in his present reduced state. No captain would ship him.

" Join the Queen's troops in India first," cried Alfred Langly. We are on the eve of some decisive battles with the Sikhs, there's no doubt of it, and loads of prize money will be obtained. You might try it just for a campaign, line your purse, and then get sent home as an invalided soldier."

Now William was weak and ill in mind and body, or he never would have listened to so unwise a proposal. Langly was always urging it; not that he had any sinister motive; he believed he was advising for the best. A person, by dint of long-continued argument, all on one side, may be persuaded into believing that " black's white ;" and in an evil hour William consented to the scheme, to try it "just for a campaign." The vision presented to his eyes—that of going home with money in his pockets and good broad-cloth on his back —was undoubtedly fascinating. The having to arrive at Whittermead in the " wretchedest old pea-jacket and patched trousers," had long been a sore upon his mind.

A detachment of one of her Majesty's regiments, the one to which Langly belonged, had been sent down to Calcutta ; and William Allair enlisted in it. It was departing to join the main army, then on the eve of encountering the Sikhs at Moultan.

You have heard of the Sikhs and our furious battles with them. They were a peaceable race of men once —not unlike the people we in England call Quakers ; but certain religious persecutions from the Mohameds and Hindoos drove them to rebellion. They inhabited the Punjaub, or land of five waters, on the western side of the Sutlej, its capital Lahore. Their king, Runjeet Singh, had the good sense to conciliate the favour of the British Government in India ; although he cast his longing eyes to the kingdom of the Sikhs on the eastern side of the Sutlej, thinking how much he should like to unite it with his own. But it was not to be attempted, for those Sikhs were under the special protection of the British.

There was peace so long as Runjeet Singh lived, but not for long after that. In December 1845, the Sikhs, whose monarch was then a puny boy, named Dhuleep Singh, crossed the Sutlej, and formed themselves into camp at Ferozeshah, intending to attack our troops. A desperate battle was fought at Moodkee, the British forces being commanded by Sir Hugh Gough, seconded by Sir John Littler. We won, of course; but it was a well-contested battle. The next engagement was fought at Ferozepore. The Governor-General of India, Sir Henry Hardinge, joined himself to the army; and, laying aside his honours as Governor-General, fought under Sir Hugh Gough. The Sikhs were thoroughly defeated, and it was supposed they had had enough of fighting—as Gruff Jones had of the sea.

In 1848 they again ventured to give us some trouble. And in December began the siege of the city of Moultan, their stronghold. They made a desperate resistance, and the fight lasted many days. It was at last taken by storm. There ensued some disastrous skirmishes at a place called Ramnugger, and then came the dreadful battle of Chillianwallah. You must all have heard of *that*.

William Allair arrived at Moultan during its siege. He had discovered that he was quite as unfitted for a soldier's life as he had been for a sailor's. Forced marches in the dreadful heat, no water, no refreshment until the end of the march—when, perhaps, they would have to wait hours before their rations, tents, and baggage could arrive—told upon *him*. An enormous number of camels was required to carry the baggage of the army: it was in the proportion of one camel to two men. Each animal was fastened by the nostril to the tail of the one preceding him; and this unwieldy train, with its native attendants, actually extended over more than fifteen miles, its progress being about a mile and a half an hour. You need not wonder that they got in a day too late for the fair, or that the exhausted men grew ill, waiting for the sustenance they so much needed. The poor patient animals were often shamefully overladen—it was the last feather, thought William, that broke the camel's back. When one of them toppled over, his load was distributed among the rest; and they, being already laden to the very extreme ounce that they could bear, would often, with the additional weight, fall also, thereby producing no end of confusion.

On the morning of the 12th January 1849, under the command of General Lord Gough, formerly Sir Hugh, the whole army moved from Lusooree to Dinghee. On the 13th, at half-past seven, they again marched on, the field hospital stores being in the rear of the heavy guns. *The field hospital stores!* In the course of a few hours, hundreds of those men, marching in health and strength, required their aid, whilst others were beyond that, and all other aid, for ever. Towards mid-day they came upon the encampment of the Sikhs. It was on the left bank of the Jhelum, on rising ground behind the jungle, the name of the place Chillianwallah, and said to be the very spot on which occurred the battle between Porus and Alexander the Great, two thousand years before.

Unwisely, our men, fatigued with their march, were hurried into battle: far better that they had been allowed to wait until the following day. It might have been so; for we were the attackers—not the Sikhs. Weary, travel-worn, hungry, thirsty, unrefreshed, the British troops were forced into action, without plan, without order.

And an awful butchery of human life it was, that same battle of Chillianwallah! It lasted from two o'clock until dark, a hand-to-hand fight, sword meeting sword, bayonet meeting bayonet. About four o'clock the British were hemmed in on all sides, and their artillery was firing to the front, to the rear, and to the flanks. Guns were taken and re-taken, colours captured and lost. Roar, and din, and confusion reigned around. The roll of the musketry deepened; the thunder of the cannonading grew louder; the bullets of the enemy whizzed about like hailstones; while, mingling with the shouts and noise of the combatants, came the shrieks of the wounded and the groans of the dying. Ever and anon, above the roar of the tempest, the hoarse voice of some commander would be heard— "Men of the ——— Europeans, prepare to charge. Charge!"

"How do you like it, Allair?" exclaimed Langly, who fought by William's side. "It's the hottest work *I* ever was in. Those Sikhs fight like demons."

"And our men like bull-dogs," was William's brief reply.

"Have your eyes about you!" exclaimed Langly, hurriedly. "Unless I am mistaken, they are bearing down upon us, sword in hand. Poor Hill!" he continued as a soldier fell at his side: "that was a fatal bullet for you! There fall two officers! Heavens! how they are swept down! Can you see who they are, Allair?"

William turned his eyes; but before he could answer, something fell in his path. It was Langly, shot down to death.

There was no stopping, and William was hurried on. He was an eye-witness to the dreadful slaughter in the Queen's 24th regiment. On they came, at full speed, this ill-fated corps : but, what could that handful do against the numbers that overwhelmed them ? The Sikhs were like ferocious beasts of prey, howling, swearing, dealing death with their deadly weapons. The unhappy 24th were exposed to it all ; to the full sweep of their batteries, the full play of their musketry. Man after man fell, officer after officer ; half the regiment was cut down in a few minutes, and the rest were falling. Two hundred lay dead, three hundred wounded —only in this one ill-fated regiment.

But, who is this who advances, sword in hand, gallantly leading on his men to avenge the death of so many of his comrades ? It is Brigadier Pennycuick ; as brave and honourable a soldier as ever drew breath. William Allair knew him well, and recognised him ; for, let me tell you, that in a scene such as this it is not so easy to recognise individuals as it is on the quiet field of peace. He had fought in many a campaign, but this was to be his last. Almost as William looked, he was struck down, sent to follow his companions, who were already standing before God. The Sikhs, with their mutilating weapons, and the Brigadier's own men, began to contend for the body.

But now another flies up, and plants himself astride on the dead Brigadier. His hand grasps his drawn sword, and he waves it nobly ; but his heart is rent, for the dead whom he would guard is his father. It was indeed the brave old officer's son ; a noble boy, younger by three years than William. But recently had he quitted England, full of hope, and in the highest spirits. And it was to run this brief career that he had come to India! Brave lad! His spirit was good to defend his father against them all; but the Sikhs would not let the boy escape with life. He fell under their weapons; and the two, father and son, were left lying on the battle-field together.

The dead and the dying lay in heaps upon the ground. Numbers, who might have been saved by surgical care and assistance, were left alone to die. And for this there was no help. Night stopped the carnage. And then William, with others, helped to do what he could for the wounded. It was a fearful task; one to make a strong man's heart shrink. They lay, writhing in their agony; not a surgeon to be had, not a taste of water! There was no linen to bandage up their wounds; there were no pillows to place their beating heads upon, save the dead men and horses that strewed the earth around them. How do you think *you* would like to make one on a battle-field?

After a while William Allair, thoroughly exhausted, lay down on the field. But not to sleep. A more dreadful night he never passed; he almost wished for a return of his delirium and the miserable forecastle of the "Prosperous." He had been slightly wounded in his left hand; it pained him much, though it was nothing to look at; and he felt ready to perish with the intense thirst. Tremblingly alive was he to the horrible details around him; not only to the multitude of dead. The wails of the dying were ringing in his ears; the in-cessant cry for water; the anguished prayer from the wounded, not to be left there, amidst the dead, to die.

Another feature of discomfort was soon added to the scene. A thick, drizzling rain came on, wetting to the skin, and putting William in mind of the perpetual soaking he had experienced in rounding Cape Horn. He rose from the ground at length, and wandered about, not openly complaining—he never did that,—but bitterly deploring the wild infatuation which had led him to quit his home for scenes such as these. Never was his folly more present to him than on this dreadful night.

Without knowing it, he came upon the field hospital. And he never forgot the sight presented to his view. Poor, poor men! poor, sick, disabled soldiers! They were lying on the ground with little help; medical attendance was lamentably scarce, and the hospital apparatus was not there! Awful suffering witnessed he that night. One incessant cry went up around — " Water! water! water!" And there was none.

Who gained the victory? We claimed it, and the Sikhs claimed it. One thing was certain—that we lost standards and guns, and did not hold the field of battle. The following morning Lord Gough rode round, in the midst of the rain, and gave orders to mark out an encampment. At four o'clock the funeral of the officers took place. William attended it. Thirteen of the ill-fated 24th were buried in one grave; Brigadier Penny-cuick and his son were buried in another.

A day or two later, William was in the hospital, waiting to have his hand dressed. He felt languid and feverish; and clinging to him was a presentiment that he should never leave the plains of India alive. It was singular that this idea should have come to him. He had escaped unhurt—or all but unhurt—from that desperate battle. Why then should a fear of death follow him now? It cannot be said why. These things are unaccountable. But the presentiment did haunt him.

Whilst he was waiting, the chaplain, the Reverend Mr Whiting, entered, and prepared to administer the sacrament of the Lord's Supper to the dying, and to others who might wish for its consolation. For the first time in his life William Allair partook of it. Few but did. The scenes gone through lately had brought men to their senses; the worst and most callous of them had become alive to the awful consideration that he possessed an immortal soul, to be welcomed or rejected by Heaven.

William knelt there with the rest, humbly repentant. His eyes were blinded with tears, his heart was riven with sorrow; and when he rose up, he dared to hope his sinful disobedience had been forgiven, and that, should it be his fate to die on those battle plains, he might sink to rest in calm trust and peace.

CHAPTER XVIII.

WILLIAM ALLAIR lingered in the hospital, willing to bestow his services, where so many were in need. He was standing close by the side of one who had received a wound in the leg, less dangerous than painful. He was a remarkably well-grown young man, six feet two inches high, and not above a year or two, as William judged, older than himself.

William fell into a train of thought. A comrade had called this young man " Jenniker," and the name had brought up vivid memories of home. Was it possible that the wounded soldier, stretched there before him, could be the once intimate companion of his boyhood? He had entered the army, and had gone out to India. William scanned him attentively, and decided in the negative; for, in the darkened, bronzed face lying there, across which a contraction of pain often passed, he could not trace the fair features of the careless schoolboy. But William might have remembered that since they met, the years which change the boy into the man had passed.

"Lend a hand to put this precious leg of mine straight, will you, comrade?" he exclaimed, suddenly addressing William.

"You are from England," William remarked, as he assisted him.

"Merry England, as they call it," was the answer. "Not that I found it so merry, or I should not have taken wing from it. Though, with all its faults, it was a decided improvement upon this."

It was certainly Jenniker. The words were characteristic of him.

"You are from Whittermead! You are Richard Jenniker!" cried William eagerly, as he laid hold of his hand.

"And who the wonder are you?" demanded Jenniker, partially raising himself on his elbows, and regarding William from top to toe.

"Do you not remember me?"

"I never saw you."

"Indeed you have, hundreds of times. We passed years at Dr Robertson's together."

"Then I have forgotten you out and out. Were you to tell me your name I should not recognise it."

"Yes, yes, you would. You have not forgotten William Allair, any more than I have forgotten Richard Jenniker."

They remained silent for some minutes, their hands locked together, each one examining the face of the other.

"I trace your features now," cried Jenniker. "But you are much altered. How broad you have got in the shoulders!"

"My service at sea has done that for me."

"And how you stoop!"

"So would you, if you had had nothing but a high chest to sit upon for three years. Going to sea spoils the figure, if it spoils nothing else, Jenniker."

Jenniker laughed. "I heard you were gone off on a pleasure trip to the Mexican coast; or enjoying the genial climate of the Polar regions. Who would have dreamt of seeing you here?"

William explained in a few words. That he had been shipwrecked, was rescued, and carried to Calcutta, where he had joined the British troops.

"What utter fools we were!" burst forth Jenniker. "Self-willed, lamentable fools! To leave England, where we might have lived in ease and plenty, and blindly embark on the perils of an untried, unknown life! I'll tell you what I have been tempted to compare it to, Allair; to the madness of those unhappy wretches, who rush, uncalled, from this world to the next. *They* know not the soundings they enter upon, neither did we."

William groaned in spirit. His "soundings" had, indeed, been false.

"But, Allair, there was one excuse for me, which you had not—if an excuse can ever be found for decamping away in disobedience. You had a jolly home and loving friends: I had neither."

"Too true."

"I had an uncle, who did not care a straw for me; a step-aunt, who hated me. The only being who ever cast a thought to me was Mildred. With a father and mother, such as you possessed, I should have been another sort of chap. It would not have been Dick Jenniker the scapegrace, but Richard Jenniker the affectionate, dutiful son Don't look so incredulous, Allair: *it would.*"

"I am not incredulous," replied William. "At the

time of your leaving, many persons spoke out plainly, and condemned Mr Jenniker for his harshness. Lord Sayingham told him of it to his face. He said you ought to have been bought off."

"Oughts don't go for much in this world. He *was* harsh to me! I wrote to him soon after I got out here; it was just after—the writing, I mean—our engagements with those demons of Sikhs at Moodkee and Ferozeshah, in 1845. Precious hot work they were, those actions; and I had the luck of arriving just in time for both. I was wounded at Ferozeshah; and while I was lying ill, not knowing, and perhaps not caring, whether I should live or die, I wrote to my uncle a letter of contrition. Begging pardon—or something akin to it—for my ungrateful escapade, and expressing a hope that if I lived to return to Europe, we might be better friends and relatives than we had ever been. Not a word spoke I of my soldier's life; that I did not find it altogether a bed of roses; and I don't suppose it would have elicited any sympathy if I had. Well, would you believe it, Allair?—he never answered the letter! He has never given me a condescending line since I left."

"Perhaps he did not receive your letter," said William.

"I know he did," was the answer. "And that they flung it aside as they had flung me—a thing unworthy of notice. Mildred writes to me; but she has to do it on the sly. A sweet, gentle girl is she! and there was more friendship between us than the world knew of. She did not think me all bad, and I deemed her the most estimable of human beings!"

" Then—if you correspond with Mildred—you must know all the news of Whittermead!" burst forth William.

" She gives me the tops and tails of it. What of that?"

" Oh, tell me!—let me hear!—what do you know of home; my home?" he exclaimed, in painful excitement.

Jenniker looked at him, and hesitated. " When did you hear last?" he questioned.

" I have never heard since I left."

" Never heard!"

" How could I hear, blocked up on that remote Californian coast? The vessel or two that did come out there, sported the stars and the stripes. At any rate, if letters came, I never got them."

" Then you are in ignorance of—of anything that may have transpired since you left?" returned Jenniker, who was looking rather subdued.

" Very nearly so. I saw Harry Vane in Calcutta. I was in the hospital, and discovered by accident that he was on board a vessel lying in the Ganges. He could not tell me much. He had not been home since he left, neither had he recently heard. The ' Hercules ' had been at New South Wales, and he supposed his letters had miscarried. It was fifteen months, full, since he had had news. How were they all at home, when Mildred last wrote?"

Jenniker made no reply. He was a bad adept at deception, fond as he used to be of the romancing—as William had once called it—with which he used to cram the school. William saw that there was something to be told which Jenniker did not like to tell. To one of quick imagination, this sort of suspense is next to unbearable. A sensation as of death-sickness came over his heart, but he maintained an outward calmness. Those who feel the most deeply show it least.

"I see you have some bad news to tell me, Jenniker. Let me know the worst at once."

Jenniker still hesitated. He did not much relish the task before him.

"You are making me ill," murmured William. "Why don't you speak out? I have strength to bear it, whatever it may be. Are—are my father and mother dead?"

"One of them," answered Jenniker, in a low voice.

"My father thought his life would not be a long one," returned William, battling with his suspense.

"When I last heard Mr Allair was ill."

"And my mother?"

"She is dead."

There was a silence. William's face was white and rigid as marble.

"What did she die of?" he presently asked.

"It was said of a broken heart."

A broken heart! The perspiration broke out, in drops as large as peas, over his livid features.

"I see it all!" he said. "My conduct killed her. In my dreams this has been sometimes shadowed forth."

"Now, don't think worse of it than it was!" cried Jenniker, glad that the ice was broken. "She went off like a person in a decline. I don't believe in broken hearts, for my part; they are all moonshine, and double moonshine. She loved you dearly, Allair, and called

M

upon you to the last. So, how could you have killed her ?"

"Called upon me to the last," echoed William, with the air of one who repeats what he does not hear.

"Mildred wrote me all about it ; she was stopping there at the time, with your sisters," continued Jenniker. "For three days previous to her death, she was scarcely in her right mind ; it was that wandering, I conclude, that sometimes precedes it. Her whole talk, then, was of you ; now praying that you might be preserved on the sea, now fancying she saw you in danger of shipwreck, and crying wildly to the sailors to save you. Next, she would witness you in all imaginary hardships, and lament, in the most heartrending terms, that you were exposed to such ; again she would fancy you had returned, and that she was clasping you in her arms, wild with joy and thankfulness, sobbing hysterically."

"Go on : tell it all," said William, for Jenniker had stopped.

"But in all her illness, in this wandering, or previous to it, she never breathed against you a word of reproach ; you were still her darling William ; her eldest and dearest child. But they said she never held up her head, so to speak, from the night you left ; and after the receipt of a letter you wrote from America, her health visibly declined.

William made no reply. He only wiped the moisture from his brow.

"In this letter, as Mildred related it to me, you said you were working on an American trading ship, and were bound for California, round Cape Horn. Now, of all dreadful accounts that anybody could give or imagine, of what the life was on board these ships, Gruff Jones gave the worst to Mrs Allair. Like an idiot, as he was, for his pains!"

"He told truth; — it is the worst," interrupted William.

"Well, he need not have said it. It couldn't improve things for you, and it only made her worry and fret over them. Let him go open-mouthed with his tale to all the village, had he liked, but he might have had the sense to spare Mrs Allair. Gruff always was a booby. Why couldn't he have persuaded her that the trading ships were little models of Paradise, where the chaps had nothing to do but sit cross-legged all day, and dine on beefsteak and onions?"

Jenniker stopped again, but still William never spoke.

"She had imagined the life dark enough before, but Gruff's description was the climax. Always was she brooding over the hardships you must undergo, the perils you were exposed to. Not that she said much; but they could see how it was. And, from what escaped her in the death-delirium, it was evident that these sorrows had haunted her night and day. Added to which, was the constant fear, or presentiment if you like, that you would not live to return."

"When did she die?" questioned William, burying his face in his hands.

"About twelve months ago, I think; but I am a bad one to remember dates. Stay—it was in January; for I know in the same letter, Mildred told me how they kept up Christmas at the Jennikers'. Yes, a twelvemonth ago, as near as possible."

"Two whole years and some months of sorrow, of yearning, for me!" he gasped. "And this is true!"

"True!" echoed Jenniker, taking the words as a question. "I shouldn't give it you if it were not true."

"How was my father?"

"Ailing," Mildred said; "not over strong."

"And the rest?" he continued, his face still hid in his hands.

"Oh, the rest were all well," carelessly replied Jenniker. "Edmund as silly as ever."

"I will come in another time, Richard," said William, starting up. But Jenniker caught him by the hand.

"Don't take it to heart in this way, Allair. Fathers and mothers must die, and it's only in the course of nature that they should go before we do. I lost mine when I was a lad. Don't take it so much to heart!"

William wrung his hand; and, without a word—for he could not utter it—made his way from the field hospital.

And when the shades of night fell and shielded him from observation, he threw himself on the ground, and sobbed aloud, in his excess of grief. The rain was falling in torrents, the earth was soaked with it, for it had scarcely ceased since the night of the battle. But he was unmindful of rain. His cup of sorrow was indeed full; and he would have been thankful to die on the spot, as he lay there. Never had the consequence of his folly, in all its sad reality, come home to him until now. His best friend on earth was gone; had broken her heart for him; had called upon him in dying: and he was far away, and knew it not.

Was it for *this* that he had passed through his dangers and his sorrows? Through the hard work on the coast; through the harder life at sea; through the fever and delirium; through the fatigue of the forced marches; through the horrors of the battle-field! Against all had his spirit fought; for there was ever a still small hope alive in his heart, whispering him to bear up, that he might once more behold the mother whose love he had so wantonly cast aside. And now he knew that that mother had died; and died for him!

Bury your face in the wet earth, William Allair, and call in vain upon her who is no longer on earth to respond. The sin of a child's ingratitude is a grievous one; and grievous must be its retribution.

CHAPTER XIX.

BOTH the Sikhs and the British forces remained some three weeks at Chillianwallah, in the position each had taken up after the battle. Then the Sikhs moved away in the night towards Goojerat, a town situated seventeen miles distant, midway between the Jhelum and the Chenab. They took possession of the place, and entrenched themselves round about it.

Lord Gough followed them, marching up his troops. I wonder if you have a tolerably correct idea of what marching in India is? It is essentially different from marching in England. Weary work it is there—killing work sometimes. They have often to push through plains of thick jungle breast high; or they plod over the hot sand, the small dust from which flies into their eyes, blinding them for the time, and causing intolerable pain. For a change, the land will be a marshy swamp, and they must wade through that. In those forced marches the burning sun seems to be a very fire, oppressing the brain, blistering the face, scorching them through their hot, heavy clothing. And there's not a drop of water to be obtained, did you give your life for it.

William Allair's hand did not heal. It gave him great pain, and became suddenly much worse; greatly inflamed and swollen. This was after the march of the troops to Goojerat, where they encamped in front of the Sikhs. The medical staff ordered William to lie by: they did not like the look of his hand at all; and a whisper went round amongst them, that locked-jaw might supervene. Wound or no wound, he was certainly very ill. During the last month his spirits had alarmingly sunk, and he was worn to a skeleton.

On the morning of the 21st of February, at sunrise, the troops got under arms, and formed up in order of battle. Lord Gough cantered down the lines, each regiment cheering him as he passed. The men and officers generally were in high spirits, chatty and cordial: an acquaintance, who at another time would be passed with a bare nod, is met with a warm grasp of the hand, when there is a chance that that day's salutation may be the last.

A little before eight, the bugles sounded the advance. A shout, that made the plain ring, broke from the entire army, as it moved on in answer. The morning was clear and beautiful, the landscape most fair, the land rich with cultivation. Between columns of infantry, their scarlet uniforms dazzling the eye, stalked the elephants, drawing the heavy guns. Dividing the divisions of infantry, went a light field battery; and between each brigade rode a troop of horse artillery, in their handsome dresses of dark blue. To the flanks rode the cavalry, some in quiet French grey, some in the sparkling costumes peculiar to the dragoons and lancers; while the irregular cavalry favoured all colours: flaming yellow, bright green, sky blue, scarlet and gold. And this beautiful scene was soon to be marred by war.

The action commenced immediately, and for three hours raged incessantly—the guns booming, the balls from either side ploughing up the earth, shattering those who stood on it. Doolie after doolie, long lines of them, passed in procession, bearing the wounded to the field hospital. Towards mid-day the battle ceased —not the slaying. The Sikhs had lost; they were flying helter skelter from the field, and the British bore down upon them, striking and slaying without quarter or mercy. They were hewn down by thousands; and those who took shelter in the village were shot or bayoneted. For ten miles did the pursuit last ; and as the British rode back to camp, it was over the numberless bodies of the slain. Charming work, that battle doing!

Strange confusion was in the camp of the Sikhs. Tumbrils and waggons were standing upside down ; the ground was strewed with the dead and dying ; wounded horses were dashing madly about in their pain ; camels and oxen danced in the rear, oversetting whatever came in their way, and turning summersets for themselves. The work of slaughter from the victorious British troops—mad then, as well as merciless— went on as hard as it could go. In this engagement we recaptured all our guns and standards lost at Chillianwallah, as well as many belonging to the enemy.

And William Allair? Was he in all this disastrous turmoil and *melée*, as he had been in that of Chillian ? No. Then where was he? In the field hospital, dying of locked-jaw. As the doctors surmised, the fatal termination had supervened.

He lay there, restless and full of pain ; yet snatching at intervals a few moments of sleep. In one of these blessed intervals there came to him the sweetest dream! All the more so, from the contrast it presented to his waking realities.

He dreamt that he was at home at Whittermead; that it was one of those brilliant, sunny days of spring, which, in spite of our railings against this unlucky climate, do condescend to visit us now and then. Just such a day as that happy 29th of May, when you met William Allair for the first time. He thought he was in the Grange meadow, lounging (it seemed too warm to run) through its growing grass, all sparkling with cowslips and bluebells, and those lilac-coloured flowers, not unlike a bluebell in shape, that they called cookoos. He vaulted over the stile—it was less trouble than to open the five-barred gate at its side—and continued his way towards Grange brook. Very soon the murmuring of the rivulet, as it ran on its course between the banks, where grew so many violets and primroses, reached his ear; and, with a pace imperceptibly quicker, he gained its side. The overhanging trees, of many sorts and sizes, cast over the stream their grateful shade—oak, ash, lime, horse-chestnut, willow, fir, larch; underneath which William had lain hundreds of times in his boyhood, gazing up through their leaves at the dark blue sky. It had puzzled the Cockney, Mr Fisher, to tell their names: it would have puzzled him still. Here, in imagination, William threw himself now, and watched the water. Nature seemed at rest. The birds were singing in the calm, quiet air, hopping from tree to tree; the butterflies and bees sported on the fragrant banks; and the ringing bells of Whittermead came flowing to his ear with the sweetest

melody, sweeter than ever he had heard it in life.
Strange that this dream should visit him amidst bodily
sufferings so great! But so it was. It was almost as
though they were for the brief moment suspended.
He seemed to lie yet on that pleasant grass. The
branches of the trees fanned the gentle breeze in his
face, and wafted onwards the faint perfume of the lime
blossoms; never had he seemed so completely to realize
the rest of earthly peace. And now, as he looked,
there knelt Edmund, in that little dell by the miniature
brick bridge; and his sisters, Alice and Rose, were
sitting on the worn old oak stump. By their side was
another form, whom he soon distinguished to be that of
Caroline Vane, with her handsome eyes and stately
presence. They were threading a daisy chain for
Edmund—as they had many a time done in reality.
A double chain, it seemed, they were going to make
him; for while Caroline Vane plucked the blossoms
from the stalks, Alice and Rose were both passing their
needles through the daisies. Suddenly he saw his
mother at his side, looking down upon him with her
gentle smile; but at the same moment a terrible thirst
came on, like that he had been forced to endure several
times of late. "Oh, mamma! I am so thirsty!" he said;
and she smiled again, and dipped a glass, which he now
saw she held in her hand, into the crystal stream of the
rivulet, through whose clearness might be seen the
white pebbles underneath. She raised it, brimming
full, and handed it to William. Whilst he was drinking, he saw his father and Harry Vane opposite to him.
The latter laughed and spoke; but William was too
agreeably occupied to listen.

He laid down the glass. It was the sweetest draught he had ever tasted: but, even while his lips were wet with its moisture, a dreadful change took place. The most frightful pain was racking him, such as he had once never imagined could be borne: the thirst he had just slaked had returned tenfold; the soft music of the bells had changed to jarring sounds; while all around him seemed to lie wounded men, soldiers, crying out with agony. For one blissful moment, William was unconscious that he had awoke to REALITY.

Oh, boys, boys! Never, never desert, as he did, your father's home. Should the temptation ever assail you, pause on the very threshold of the ill-omened thought, and remember William Allair.

One of the surgeons, Dr MacRae, came up and looked at him, for he had given vent to a sharp wail of anguish. The doctor little thought that it proceeded from the sick mind, rather than from the body. How should he think it? He passed on: nothing more could be done in this world for William Allair.

He turned his painful eyes, over which the shades of death were gathering, upon the doolies, as they were brought in with the wounded. In one of those doolies lay the fine form of Richard Jenniker. Cured of the hurt received at Chillianwallah, he had gone forth that morning, a hale, healthy man; and now he was brought back, wounded unto death.

" Lay me down here." he panted to the soldiers who bore him, indicating by a nervous motion of the hand the spot close to William. " I suppose this is our last day on earth, Allair, so we may as well die in company."

" Can nothing be done for you?" murmured William,

whose indistinct utterance and closed mouth prevented Jenniker's catching at more than the sound of the words, and he had to guess at the sense.

"Nothing, they say. I have got a big hole in the side, and the blood's welling out of me like a waterspout."

"I was in hopes you would have been spared. And would have borne back tidings of my death to Whitter-mead."

"It is decreed otherwise, it seems. By this time to-morrow, we shall both have passed into another world."

William cast his reproachful eyes towards him.

"I know what that means," cried Jenniker. "You would say that my tone of speech ill becomes such as we are. But it comes natural to me. I meant nothing wrong: nobody could at an hour like this. God is all-powerful to save. He forgives what we'd not forgive to one another. We have seen our share of ill in this life, Allair, knocked about as we have been: let us trust that, by God's mercy, which we greatly need, the next will prove a brighter and a better world for us."

"Amen!" said William, as he clasped his hands together. "Amen, Amen!"

They were both buried the next morning in the common grave, shared by the others who had died in the night. What should we all do with this world's sin, and mistakes, and suffering, but for that other blessed world which has to come!—for God's mercy, for our Saviour's love!

And now, boys, what do you think of running away to sea?

MURRAY AND GIBB, PRINTERS, EDINBURGH.

Original Juvenile Library.

A CATALOGUE

OF

NEW AND POPULAR WORKS,

PRINCIPALLY FOR YOUNG PERSONS.

Goldsmith introduced to Newbery by Dr. Johnson

PUBLISHED BY

GRIFFITH AND FARRAN,

SUCCESSORS TO

NEWBERY AND HARRIS,

CORNER OF ST. PAUL'S CHURCHYARD, LONDON.

MDCCCLXIV.

Stanesby's Illuminated Gift Books.

EVERY PAGE RICHLY PRINTED IN GOLD AND COLOURS.

THE FLORAL GIFT.
Small 4to, price 14s. cloth elegant; 21s. morocco extra.

APHORISMS OF THE WISE AND GOOD:
With a Photographic Portrait of Milton. Price 9s. cloth elegant; 14s. Turkey morocco antique.

. Printed the same size, and forming a companion to "Shakespeare's Household Words."

SHAKESPEARE'S HOUSEHOLD WORDS:
With a Photographic Portrait taken from the Monument at Stratford-on-Avon. Price 9s. cloth elegant; 14s. morocco antique.

" An exquisite little gem, fit to be the Christmas offering to Titania or Queen Mab."—*The Critic.*

THE WISDOM OF SOLOMON:
From the Book of Proverbs. With a Frontispiece representing the Queen of Sheba's Visit to Solomon. Small 4to, price 14s. cloth elegant; 18s. calf; 21s. morocco antique.

THE BRIDAL SOUVENIR:
Containing the Choicest Thoughts of the Best Authors, in Prose and Verse. New Edition, with Portrait of the PRINCESS ROYAL after Winterhalter. Elegantly bound in white and gold, price 21s.

" A splendid specimen of decorative art, and well suited for a bridal gift."—*Literary Gazette.*

THE BIRTHDAY SOUVENIR:
A Book of Thoughts on Life and Immortality. Small 4to, price 12s. 6d. illuminated cloth; 18s. morocco antique.

LIGHT FOR THE PATH OF LIFE:
From the Holy Scriptures. Small 4to, price 12s. cloth elegant; 15s. calf, gilt edges; 18s. morocco antique.

NEW BOOK OF EMBLEMS.
Square 8vo, price 21s. cloth elegant; 27s. calf extra; 31s. 6d. morocco antique. Beautifully printed by Whittingham, in Old English type, with the Initial Letters and Borders in Red.

Spiritual Conceits:
Extracted from the Writings of the Fathers, the Old English Poets, &c., with One Hundred Designs, forming Symbolical Illustrations to the passages, by W. HARRY ROGERS.

" A book full of deep thought and beautiful yet quaint artistic work."—*Art Journal.*

NEW AND POPULAR WORKS.

BY THE AUTHOR OF "MARY POWELL," ETC.

THE INTERRUPTED WEDDING:

A Hungarian Tale. With an Illustration by HENRY
WARREN. Post 8vo, price 6s., extra cloth.

MRS. HENRY WOOD'S NEW TALE FOR BOYS.

WILLIAM ALLAIR;

Or, Running Away to Sea. By the Author of "East
Lynne," "The Channings," &c. Frontispiece by F. GILBERT.
Fcap. 8vo; price 2s. 6d. cloth; 3s. gilt edges.

LADY LUSHINGTON.

THE HAPPY HOME;

Or, The Children at the Red House. By LADY LUSHING-
TON. Illustrated by G. J. PINWELL. Super-royal 16mo,
price 3s. 6d. cloth; 4s. 6d. coloured, gilt edges.

ELWES' NEW BOOK FOR BOYS.

LUKE ASHLEIGH;

Or, School Life in Holland. By ALFRED ELWES, Author
of "Guy Rivers," "Paul Blake," &c. Illustrated by G.
DU MAURIER. Fcap. 8vo, price 5s. cloth; 5s. 6d. gilt edges.

MRS. DAVENPORT.

OUR BIRTHDAYS;

And How to Improve Them. By Mrs. E. Davenport, Author of "Fickle Flora," &c. Frontispiece by D. H. Friston. Fcap. 8vo, price 2s. 6d.; cloth, 3s. gilt edges.

REV. H. P. DUNSTER.

HISTORICAL TALES OF LANCASTRIAN TIMES.

By the Rev. H. P. Dunster, M.A. With Illustrations by John Franklin. Fcap. 8vo, price 5s. cloth; 5s. 6d. gilt edges.

TINY STORIES FOR TINY READERS IN TINY WORDS.

By the Author of "Tuppy," "Triumphs of Steam," &c. With Twelve Illustrations by Weir. Super-royal 16mo, price 2s. 6d. cloth; 3s. 6d. coloured, gilt edges.

NURSERY NONSENSE;

Or, Rhymes without Reason. By D'Arcy W. Thompson. With Sixty Illustrations by C. H. Bennett. Imperial 16mo, price 2s. 6d. cloth; 4s. 6d. coloured, cloth elegant, gilt edges.

LITTLE BY LITTLE;

A Series of Graduated Lessons in the Art of Reading Music. By the Author of "Conversations on Harmony." Oblong 8vo, price 3s. 6d. cloth.

MEMORABLE BATTLES IN ENGLISH HISTORY;

Where Fought, Why Fought, and their Results, with the MILITARY LIVES OF THE COMMANDERS. By W. H. DAVENPORT ADAMS, Author of "Neptune's Heroes." Frontispiece by ROBERT DUDLEY. Post 8vo, price 7s. 6d., extra cloth.

"Of the care and honesty of the author's labours, the book gives abundant proof."—*Athenæum*.

OUR SOLDIERS;

Or, Anecdotes of the Gallant Deeds of the British Army during the reign of Her Majesty QUEEN VICTORIA. By W. H. G. KINGSTON. With Frontispiece from a painting in the Victoria Cross Gallery. Fcap. 8vo, price 3s. cloth; 3s. 6d. gilt edges.

OUR SAILORS;

Or, Anecdotes of the Gallant Deeds of the British Navy during the reign of Her Majesty QUEEN VICTORIA. With Frontispiece. Fcap. 8vo, price 3s. cloth; 3s. 6d. gilt edges.

** These volumes abundantly prove that both our officers and men in the Army and Navy have been found as ready as ever to dare and to do as were dared and done of yore, when led by a Nelson or a Wellington.

A HANDBOOK OF THE HISTORY OF THE UNITED STATES:

Including the Colonial Period, War of Independence, Constitution of the States, &c. By HUGO REID, late Principal of Dalhousie College, Halifax, Nova Scotia. Fcap. 8vo, price 2s. 6d. cloth.

MY GRANDMOTHER'S BUDGET

Of Stories and Verses. By FRANCES FREELING BRODERIP, Author of "Tiny Tadpole," &c. With Illustrations by her brother, THOMAS HOOD. Super-royal 16mo, price 3s. 6d. cloth; 4s. 6d. coloured, gilt edges.

"Some of the most charming little inventions that ever adorned this department of literature."—*Illustrated Times*.

THE LOVES OF TOM TUCKER AND LITTLE BO-PEEP.

Written and Illustrated by THOMAS HOOD. Quarto, price
2s. 6d., coloured plates.

"Full of fun and good humour. The illustrations are excellent."—*Critic.*

SCENES AND STORIES OF THE RHINE.

By M. BETHAM EDWARDS, Author of "Holidays among
the Mountains," &c. With Illustrations by F. W. KEYL.
Super-royal 16mo, price 3s. 6d. cloth; 4s. 6d. coloured,
gilt edges.

" Full of amusing incident, good stories, and sprightly pictures."—*Dial.*

NURSERY FUN:

Or the Little Folks' Picture Book. The Illustrations by C.
H. BENNETT. Quarto, price 2s. 6d., coloured plates.

" Will be greeted with shouts of laughter in any nursery."—*Critic.*

PLAY-ROOM STORIES;

Or, How to Make Peace. By GEORGIANA M. CRAIK.
With Illustrations by C. GREEN. Super-royal 16mo, price
3s. 6d. cloth; 4s. 6d. coloured, gilt edges.

" This book will come with 'peace' on its wings into many a play-
room."—*Art Journal.*

FICKLE FLORA,

And her Sea-side Friends. By EMMA DAVENPORT. Illustrated by ABSOLON. Super-royal 16mo., price 3s. 6d. cloth;
4s. 6d. coloured, gilt edges.

LIVE TOYS;

Or, Anecdotes of our Four-legged and other Pets. By
EMMA DAVENPORT. Illustrations by H. WEIR. Super-royal
16mo, price 2s. 6d. cloth; 3s. 6d. coloured, gilt edges.

" One of the best kind of books for youthful readers; its dumb heroes
have all the interest of characters in fiction."—*Guardian.*

THE FAITHFUL HOUND:

A Story in Verse founded on fact. By LADY THOMAS, with
Illustrations by H. WEIR. Imperial 16mo, price 2s. 6d.,
cloth; 3s. 6d., coloured, gilt edges.

DEDICATED TO ALFRED TENNYSON.

THE STORY OF KING ARTHUR,

And his Knights of the Round Table. Compiled and arranged by J. T. K. With Illustrations by G. H. THOMAS. Post 8vo, price 7s. cloth; 9s. coloured, gilt edges.

"The story of King Arthur will never die while there are Englishmen to study and English boys to devour its tales of adventure."—*Preface.*

CAPTAIN MARRYAT'S DAUGHTER.

HARRY AT SCHOOL.

By EMILIA MARRYAT. Illustrations by ABSOLON. Super-royal 16mo, price 2s. 6d. cloth; 3s. 6d. coloured, gilt edges.

"Really good, and fitted to delight little boys."—*Spectator.*

LONG EVENINGS;

Or, Stories for My Little Friends, by EMILIA MARRYAT. Illustrated by ABSOLON. Second Edition. Super-royal 16mo, price 2s. 6d. cloth; 3s. 6d. coloured, gilt edges.

"This book cannot fail to be a favourite."—*Art Journal.*

THOMAS HOOD'S DAUGHTER.

TINY TADPOLE,

And other Tales. By FRANCES FREELING BRODERIP. With Illustrations by her Brother, THOMAS HOOD. Super-royal 16mo, price 3s. 6d. cloth; 4s. 6d. coloured, gilt edges.

"A remarkable book, produced by the brother and sister of a family in which genius and fun are inherited."—*Saturday Review.*

DISTANT HOMES;

Or, the Graham Family in New Zealand. By Mrs. I. E. AYLMER. With Illustrations by J. JACKSON. Super-royal 16mo, price 3s. 6d. cloth; 4s. 6d. coloured, gilt edges.

"All who have the good fortune to make acquaintance with this book will derive not only amusement, but a vast amount of instruction."—*English Churchman.*

WORKS FOR BOYS, BY ALFRED ELWES.

With Illustrations, Fcap. 8vo, price 5s. cloth ; 5s. 6d. gilt edges.

GUY RIVERS;

Or, a Boy's Struggles in the Great World. Illustrations
by H. ANELAY.

"Mr. Elwes sustains his reputation. Boys will derive both pleasure and
profit from the reading of 'Guy Rivers.'"—*Athenæum.*

RALPH SEABROOKE;

Or, the Adventures of a Young Artist in Piedmont and
Tuscany. Illustrated by ROBERT DUDLEY.

"This book contains a considerable amount of interesting and amusing
description with regard to the manners and the habits of the Italians."—
Illustrated News.

FRANK AND ANDREA;

Or, Forest Life in the Island of Sardinia. Illustrated by
DUDLEY.

"The descriptions of Sardinian life and scenery are admirable."—
Athenæum.

PAUL BLAKE;

Or, The STORY of a BOY's PERILS in the ISLANDS of CORSICA
and MONTE CRISTO. Illustrated by ANELAY.

"This spirited and engaging story will lead our young friends to a very
intimate acquaintance with the island of Corsica."—*Art Journal.*

MEADOW LEA;

Or, the Gipsy Children. A Story founded on Fact. By the
Author of "The Triumphs of Steam," "Our Eastern Empire," &c. With Illustrations by JOHN GILBERT. Fcap.
8vo, price 4s. 6d. cloth ; 5s. gilt edges.

NEPTUNE'S HEROES;

Or, The Sea Kings of England ; from Hawkins to Franklin.
By W. H. D. ADAMS. Illustrated by MORGAN. Fcap.
8vo, price 5s. cloth ; 5s. 6d. gilt edges.

"We trust Old England will ever have writers as ready and able as Mr.
Adams to interpret to her children the noble lives of her greatest men."—
Athenæum.

DALTON'S BOOKS FOR BOYS.

With Illustrations, Fcap. 8vo, price 5s. cloth; 5s. 6d. gilt edges.

LOST IN CEYLON:

The Story of a Boy and Girl's Adventures in the Woods and Wilds of the Lion King of Kandy. Illustrated by WEIR.

" Clever, exciting, and full of true description."—*Spectator.*

THE WHITE ELEPHANT;

Or, the Hunters of Ava, and the King of the Golden Foot. Illustrated by HARRISON WEIR.

" Full of dash, nerve, and spirit, and withal freshness."—*Literary Gazette.*

THE WAR TIGER;

Or, ADVENTURES AND WONDERFUL FORTUNES OF THE YOUNG SEA-CHIEF AND HIS LAD CHOW. Illustrated by H. S. MELVILLE.

" A tale of lively adventure, vigorously told, and embodying much curious information."—*Illustrated News.*

THE LATE THOMAS HOOD.

FAIRY LAND;

Or, Recreation for the Rising Generation, in Prose and Verse. By the late THOMAS and JANE HOOD, their Son and Daughter, &c. Illustrated by T. HOOD, Jun. Super-royal 16mo, price 3s. 6d. cloth; 4s. 6d. coloured, gilt edges.

"These tales are charming. Before it goes into the nursery, we recommend that all grown-up people should study 'Fairy Land.'"—*Blackwood.*

THE HEADLONG CAREER AND WOFUL ENDING OF

PRECOCIOUS PIGGY. Written for his Children, by the late THOMAS HOOD. With a Preface by his Daughter; and Illustrated by his Son. Third Edition. Post 4to, price 2s. 6d. coloured ; 3s. 6d. mounted on cloth.

" The Illustrations are intensely humorous."—*The Critic.*

THE NINE LIVES OF A CAT:

A Tale of Wonder. Written and Illustrated by C. H. BENNETT. Twenty-four Engravings. Imperial 16mo, price 2s. cloth ; 2s. 6d. coloured, gilt edges.

"Rich in the quaint humour and fancy that a man of genius knows how to spare for the enlivenment of children."—*Examiner.*

LANDELLS' INSTRUCTIVE AND AMUSING WORKS.

THE BOY'S OWN TOY MAKER:

A Practical Illustrated Guide to the useful employment of Leisure Hours. By E. LANDELLS. Sixth Edition. With 200 Illustrations. Royal 16mo, price 2s. 6d. cloth.

"A new and valuable form of endless amusement."—*Nonconformist.*
"We recommend it to all who have children to be instructed and amused."—*Economist.*

THE GIRL'S OWN TOY MAKER,

And Book of Recreation. By E. and A. LANDELLS. Third Edition. With 200 Illustrations. Royal 16mo, price 2s. 6d. cloth.

"A perfect magazine of information."—*Illustrated News of the World.*

HOME PASTIME;

Or, THE CHILD'S OWN TOY MAKER. With practical instructions. By E. LANDELLS. New Edition. Price 3s. 6d. complete, with the Cards and Descriptive Letter-press.

‍‍* By this novel and ingenious "Pastime," beautiful Models can be made by Children from the Cards, by attending to the plain and simple Instructions in the Book.

"As a delightful exercise of ingenuity, and a most sensible mode of passing a winter's evening, we commend the Child's own Toy Maker."—*Illustrated News.*
"Should be in every house blessed with the presence of children."—*The Field.*

THE ILLUSTRATED PAPER MODEL MAKER:

Containing Twelve Pictorial Subjects, with Descriptive Letter-press and Diagrams for the Construction of the Models. By E. LANDELLS. Price 2s., in a neat Envelope.

"A most excellent method of educating both eye and hand in the knowledge of form."—*English Churchman.*

BLIND MAN'S HOLIDAY;

Or, Short Tales for the Nursery. By the Author of "Mia and Charlie," &c. Illustrated by ABSOLON. Super-royal 16mo, price 3s. 6d. cloth ; 4s. 6d. coloured, gilt edges.

"Very true to nature and admirable in feeling."—*Guardian.*

FUNNY FABLES FOR LITTLE FOLKS.

By FRANCES FREELING BRODERIP (Daughter of the late THOMAS HOOD). Illustrated by her Brother. Super-royal 16mo, price 2s. 6d. cloth ; 3s. 6d. coloured, gilt edges.

"The Fables contain the happiest mingling of fun, fancy, humour, and instruction."—*Art Journal.*

WORKS FOR DISTRIBUTION.

A WOMAN'S SECRET;

Or, How to Make Home Happy. Twenty-fourth Thousand. 18mo, with Frontispiece. Price 6d.

By the same Author, uniform in size and price.

WOMAN'S WORK;

Or, How she can Help the Sick. Fourteenth Thousand.

A CHAPTER OF ACCIDENTS;

Or, the Mother's Assistant in cases of Burns, Scalds, Cuts, &c. Seventh Thousand.

PAY TO-DAY, TRUST TO-MORROW:

A Story founded on Facts, illustrative of the Evils of the Tally System. Fifth Thousand.

NURSERY WORK;

Or, Hannah Baker's First Place. Fourth Thousand.

STORIES OF HOME LIFE.

Being the Four First Works as above, bound in One Volume, price 2s. 6d. cloth.

FAMILY PRAYERS FOR COTTAGE HOMES;

With a few Words on Prayer, and Select Scripture Passages. Fcap. 8vo, price 4d. limp cloth.

*** These little works are admirably adapted for circulation among the working classes.

THE TRIUMPHS OF STEAM;

Or, STORIES FROM THE LIVES OF WATT, ARKWRIGHT, AND STEPHENSON. By the Author of "Might not Right," "Our Eastern Empire," &c. With Illustrations by J. GILBERT. Dedicated by permission to the late Robert Stephenson. Second Edition. Royal 16mo, price 3s. 6d. cloth; 4s. 6d.. coloured, gilt edges.

" A most delicious volume of examples."—*Art Journal.*

MIGHT NOT RIGHT;

Or, STORIES OF THE DISCOVERY AND CONQUEST OF AMERICA. Illustrated by J. GILBERT. Royal 16mo, price 3s. 6d. cloth; 4s. 6d. coloured, and gilt edges.

" With the fortunes of Columbus, Cortes, and Pizarro, for the staple of these stories, the writer has succeeded in producing a very interesting volume."—*Illustrated News.*

HISTORY OF INDIA FOR THE YOUNG.

OUR EASTERN EMPIRE;

Or, STORIES FROM THE HISTORY OF BRITISH INDIA. With Four Illustrations. Second Edition, with continuation to the Proclamation of Queen Victoria. Royal 16mo, 3s. 6d. cloth; 4s. 6d. coloured, gilt edges.

" These stories are charming, and convey a general view of the progress of our Empire in the East. The tales are told with admirable clearness."— *Athenæum.*

THE MARTYR LAND;

Or, TALES OF THE VAUDOIS. Frontispiece by J. GILBERT. Royal 16mo, price 3s. 6d. cloth.

" While practical lessons run throughout, they are never obtruded; the whole tone is refined without affectation, religious and cheerful."—*English Churchman.*

TUPPY;

Or, the Autobiography of a Donkey. By the Author of "The Triumphs of Steam," &c. &c. Illustrated by HARRISON WEIR. Second Edition. Super-royal 16mo, price 2s. 6d. cloth; 3s. 6d. coloured, gilt edges.

" A very intelligent donkey, worthy of the distinction conferred upon him by the artist."—*Art Journal.*

HOLIDAYS AMONG THE MOUNTAINS;

Or, Scenes and Stories of Wales. By M. BETHAM EDWARDS. Illustrated by F. J. SKILL. Super-royal 16mo, price 3s. 6d. cloth; 4s. 6d. coloured, gilt edges.

"The most charming book for girls we have met with for a long time."—*Bell's Messenger.*

THE FAIRY TALES OF SCIENCE:

A Book for Youth. By J. C. BROUGH. With 16 beautiful Illustrations by C. H. BENNETT. Fcap. 8vo, price 5s. cloth.

"Science, perhaps, was never made more attractive and easy of entrance into the youthful mind."—*The Builder.*
"Altogether the volume is one of the most original, as well as one of the most useful, books of the season."—*Gentleman's Magazine.*

SUNDAY EVENINGS WITH SOPHIA;

Or, LITTLE TALKS ON GREAT SUBJECTS. A Book for Girls. By LEONORA G. BELL. With Frontispiece by J. ABSOLON. Fcap. 8vo, price 2s. 6d. cloth.

"A very suitable gift for a thoughtful girl."—*Bell's Messenger.*

SCENES OF ANIMAL LIFE AND CHARACTER:

FROM NATURE AND RECOLLECTION. In Twenty Plates. By J. B. 4to, price 2s. plain; 2s. 6d. coloured, fancy boards.

"Truer, heartier, more playful, or more enjoyable sketches of animal life could scarcely be found anywhere."—*Spectator.*

PICTORIAL GEOGRAPHY,

For the Use of Children, presenting at one View Illustrations of the various *Geographical Terms*, and thus imparting clear and definite Ideas of their Meaning. On a large sheet Imperial, price 2s. 6d., printed in tints; 5s. on roller, varnished.

HAND SHADOWS,

To be thrown upon the Wall. By HENRY BURSILL. First and Second Series, each containing Eighteen Novel and Original Designs. 4to, price 2s. each, plain; 2s. 6d. coloured.

"Uncommonly clever—some wonderful effects are produced."—*The Press.*

OLD NURSE'S BOOK OF RHYMES, JINGLES, AND DITTIES.

Edited and Illustrated by C. H. BENNETT, Author of "Shadows." With Ninety Engravings. Fcap. 4to, price 3s. 6d. cloth, plain, or 6s. coloured.

"The illustrations are all so replete with fun and imagination, that we scarcely know who will be most pleased with the book, the good-natured grandfather who gives it, or the chubby grandchild who gets it, for a Christmas-Box."—*Notes and Queries.*

BERRIES AND BLOSSOMS:

A Verse Book for Young Children. By T. WESTWOOD. With coloured Frontispiece and Title. Super-royal 16mo, price 3s. 6d. gilt edges.

THE GRATEFUL SPARROW.

A True Story. Third Edition, with Frontispiece. Price 6d. sewed.

HOW I BECAME A GOVERNESS.

By the Author of "The Grateful Sparrow." With Frontispiece. Price 1s. sewed.

DICKY BIRDS.

A True Story, by the Author of "The Grateful Sparrow." With Frontispiece. Price 6d.

JACK FROST AND BETTY SNOW;

WITH OTHER TALES FOR WINTRY NIGHTS AND RAINY DAYS. Illustrated by H. WEIR. 2s. 6d. cloth; 3s. 6d. coloured, gilt edges.

"The dedication of these pretty tales proves by whom they are written; they are indelibly stamped with that natural and graceful method of amusing while instructing which only persons of genius possess."—*Art Journal.*

MAUD SUMMERS THE SIGHTLESS:

A NARRATIVE FOR THE YOUNG. Illustrated by ABSOLON. 3s. 6d. cloth; 4s. 6d. coloured, gilt edges.

"A touching and beautiful story."—*Christian Treasury.*

CLARA HOPE;

Or, THE BLADE AND THE EAR. By MISS MILNER. With Frontispiece by BIRKET FOSTER. Fcap. 8vo, price 3s. 6d. cloth; 4s. 6d. cloth elegant, gilt edges.

"A beautiful narrative, showing how bad habits may be eradicated, and evil tempers subdued."—*British Mother's Journal.*

THE ADVENTURES AND EXPERIENCES OF BIDDY

DORKING, AND OF THE FAT FROG. Edited by MRS. S. C. HALL. Illustrated by H. WEIR. 2s. 6d. cloth; 3s. 6d. coloured, gilt edges.

"Most amusingly and wittily told."—*Morning Herald.*

HISTORICAL ACTING CHARADES;

Or, AMUSEMENTS FOR WINTER EVENINGS. By the Author of "Cat and Dog," &c. New Edition. Fcap. 8vo, price 3s. 6d. cloth; 4s. gilt edges.

"A rare book for Christmas parties, and of practical value."—*Illustrated News.*

THE STORY OF JACK AND THE GIANTS,

With Thirty-five Illustrations by RICHARD DOYLE. Beautifully printed. New and Cheaper Edition. Fcap. 4to, price 2s. 6d. cloth; 3s. 6d. coloured, cloth, gilt edges.

"In Doyle's drawings we have wonderful conceptions, which will secure the book a place amongst the treasures of collectors, as well as excite the imaginations of children."—*Illustrated Times.*

THE EARLY DAWN;

Or, STORIES TO THINK ABOUT. By a COUNTRY CLERGYMAN. Illustrated by H. WEIR, &c. Small 4to, price 2s. 6d. cloth; 3s. 6d. coloured, gilt edges.

"The matter is both wholesome and instructive, and must fascinate as well as benefit the young."—*Literarium.*

ANGELO;

Or, THE PINE FOREST AMONG THE ALPS. By GERALDINE E. JEWSBURY, Author of "The Adopted Child," &c. With Illustrations by JOHN ABSOLON. Small 4to, price 2s. 6d. cloth; 3s. 6d. coloured, gilt edges.

"As pretty a child's story as one might look for on a winter's day."—*Examiner.*

GRANNY'S WONDERFUL CHAIR;

AND ITS TALES OF FAIRY TIMES. By FRANCES BROWNE. With Illustrations by KENNY MEADOWS. Small 4to, 3s. 6d. cloth; 4s. 6d. coloured, gilt edges.

"One of the happiest blendings of marvel and moral we have ever seen."—*Literary Gazette.*

THE HISTORY OF A QUARTERN LOAF.

Rhymes and Pictures. By WILLIAM NEWMAN. 12 Illustrations. Price 6d. plain, 1s. coloured; or mounted on linen and bound in cloth, 2s. 6d.

Uniform in size and price.

THE HISTORY OF A SCUTTLE OF COALS.

THE HISTORY OF A CUP OF TEA.

THE HISTORY OF A LUMP OF SUGAR.

THE HISTORY OF A BALE OF COTTON. (Just published.)

THE HISTORY OF A GOLDEN SOVEREIGN. (Just published.)

*** The Loaf, Tea, and Sugar bound in one volume, cloth, 2s. plain, 3s. 6d. coloured; also Sugar, Cotton, and Gold, in one volume, same price.

———

FAGGOTS FOR THE FIRESIDE;

Or, TALES OF FACT AND FANCY. By PETER PARLEY. Twelve Tinted Illustrations. New Edition. Fcap. 8vo, 3s. 6d. cloth; 4s. 6d. coloured.

"A new work by Peter Parley is a pleasant greeting for all boys and girls, wherever the English language is spoken or read. He has a happy method of conveying information, while seeming to address himself to the imagination."—*The Critic.*

THE DISCONTENTED CHILDREN;

AND HOW THEY WERE CURED. By MARY and ELIZ. KIRBY. Illustrated by H. K. BROWNE (Phiz). Second Edition, price 2s. 6d. cloth; 3s. 6d. coloured, gilt edges.

" We know no better method of banishing 'discontent' from school-room and nursery than by introducing this wise and clever story to their inmates."—*Art Journal.*

THE TALKING BIRD;

Or, THE LITTLE GIRL WHO KNEW WHAT WAS GOING TO HAPPEN. By M. and E. KIRBY. With Illustrations by H. K. BROWNE. Price 2s. 6d. cloth; 3s. 6d. coloured.

"The story is ingeniously told, and the moral clearly shown."
Athenæum.

JULIA MAITLAND;

Or, PRIDE GOES BEFORE A FALL. By M. and E. KIRBY. Illustrated by JOHN ABSOLON. Price 2s. 6d. cloth; 3s. 6d. coloured, gilt edges.

" It is nearly such a story as Miss Edgeworth might have written on the same theme."—*The Press.*

TALES OF MAGIC AND MEANING.

Written and Illustrated by ALFRED CROWQUILL. Price 3s. 6d. cloth ; 4s. 6d. coloured, gilt edges.

" Cleverly written and abounding in frolic and pathos, and inculcating so pure a moral, that we must pronounce him a very fortunate little fellow who catches these ' Tales of Magic ' from a Christmas-tree."—*Athenæum*.

THE REMARKABLE HISTORY OF THE HOUSE THAT

JACK BUILT. Splendidly Illustrated and magnificently Illuminated by THE SON OF A GENIUS. Price 2s., *in fancy cover*.

" Magnificent in suggestion, and most comical in expression."—*Athenæum*.

LETTERS FROM SARAWAK,

Addressed to a Child. Embracing an Account of the Manners, Customs, and Religion of the Inhabitants of Borneo, with Incidents of Missionary Life. By MRS. M'DOUGALL. Fourth Thousand, with Illustrations. 3s. 6d. cloth.

" All is new, interesting, and admirably told."—*Church and State Gazette*.

COMICAL PICTURE BOOKS.

Uniform in size with " The Struwwelpeter."

PICTURE FABLES.

Written and Illustrated by ALFRED CROWQUILL. Sixteen large coloured Plates. Price 2s. 6d. fancy boards.

THE CARELESS CHICKEN.

By the BARON KRAKEMSIDES. With Sixteen large coloured Plates, by ALFRED CROWQUILL. 4to, 2s. 6d. fancy boards.

FUNNY LEAVES FOR THE YOUNGER BRANCHES.

By the BARON KRAKEMSIDES of Burstenoudelafen Castle. Illustrated by ALFRED CROWQUILL. Coloured Plates. 2s. 6d.

LAUGH AND GROW WISE.

By the SENIOR OWL of Ivy Hall. With Sixteen Large Coloured Plates. 4to, price 2s. 6d. fancy boards.

. Mounted on cloth, 1s. each extra.

A 6

PEEP AT THE PIXIES;

Or, LEGENDS OF THE WEST. By MRS. BRAY, Author of "Life of Stothard," &c. Illustrations by H. K. BROWNE (Phiz). Price 3s. 6d. cloth; 4s. 6d. coloured, gilt edges.

"A peep at the actual Pixies of Devonshire, faithfully described by Mrs. Bray, is a treat. Her knowledge of the locality, her affection for her subject, her exquisite feeling for nature, and her real delight in fairy lore, have given a freshness to the little volume we did not expect. The notes at the end contain matter of interest for all who feel a desire to know the origin of such tales and legends."—*Art Journal.*

OCEAN AND HER RULERS;

A Narrative of the Nations who have from the Earliest Ages held dominion over the Sea; comprising a brief History of Navigation, from the remotest Periods to the Present Time. By ALFRED ELWES. Fcap. 8vo, 5s. cloth.

"The volume is replete with valuable and interesting information; and we cordially recommend it as a useful auxiliary in the school-room, and entertaining companion in the library."—*Morning Post.*

A BOOK FOR EVERY CHILD.

THE FAVOURITE PICTURE-BOOK:

A Gallery of Delights, designed for the Amusement and Instruction of the Young. With several hundred Illustrations from Drawings by J. ABSOLON, H. K. BROWNE (Phiz), J. GILBERT, T. LANDSEER, J. LEECH, J. S. PROUT, H. WEIR, &c. New Edition. Royal 4to, price 3s. 6d. bound in a new and elegant cover; 7s. 6d. coloured; 10s. 6d. coloured and mounted on cloth.

THE DAY OF A BABY-BOY:

A Story for a Little Child. By E. BERGER, with Illustrations by JOHN ABSOLON. Second Edition. Super-royal 16mo, price 2s. 6d. cloth; 3s. 6d. coloured, gilt edges.

"A sweet little book for the nursery."—*Christian Times.*

CAT AND DOG;

Or, MEMOIRS OF PUSS AND THE CAPTAIN. A Story founded on Fact. Illustrated by HARRISON WEIR. Sixth Edition. Super-royal 16mo, 2s. 6d. cloth; 3s. 6d. coloured, gilt edges.

"The author of this amusing little tale is evidently a keen observer of nature. The illustrations are well executed; and the moral which points the tale is conveyed in the most attractive form."—*Britannia.*

THE DOLL AND HER FRIENDS;

Or, MEMOIRS OF THE LADY SERAPHINA. By the Author of "Cat and Dog." Third Edition. With Four Illustrations by H. K. BROWNE (Phiz). Small 4to, 2s. 6d. cloth; 3s. 6d. coloured, gilt edges.

"Evidently written by one who has brought great powers to bear upon a small matter."—*Morning Herald.*

CLARISSA DONNELLY;

Or, THE HISTORY OF AN ADOPTED CHILD. By GERALDINE E. JEWSBURY. With an Illustration by JOHN ABSOLON. Fcap. 8vo, 3s. 6d. cloth; 4s. gilt edges.

"With wonderful power, only to be matched by as admirable a simplicity, Miss Jewsbury has narrated the history of a child. For nobility of purpose, for simple, nervous writing, and for artistic construction, it is one of the most valuable works of the day."—*Lady's Companion.*

FAMILIAR NATURAL HISTORY.

With Forty-two Illustrations by HARRISON WEIR, and descriptive letter-press by Mrs. R. LEE. Price 3s. 6d. cloth, plain; 5s. coloured, gilt edges.

HARRY HAWKINS'S H-BOOK;

SHOWING HOW HE LEARNED TO ASPIRATE HIS H'S. Frontispiece by WEIR. Second Edition, price 6d.

"No family or schoolroom within, or indeed beyond, the sound of Bow bells, should be without this merry manual."—*Art Journal.*

THE FAMILY BIBLE NEWLY OPENED;

WITH UNCLE GOODWIN'S ACCOUNT OF IT. By JEFFERYS TAYLOR, Author of "A Glance at the Globe," &c. Frontispiece by J. GILBERT. Fcap. 8vo, 3s. 6d. cloth.

"A very good account of the Sacred Writings, adapted to the taste, feelings, and intelligence of young people."—*Educational Times.*

"Parents will also find it a great aid in the religious teaching of their families."—*Edinburgh Witness.*

KATE AND ROSALIND;

Or, EARLY EXPERIENCES. By the Author of "Quicksands on Foreign Shores," &c. Fcap. 8vo, 3s. 6d. cloth; 4s. gilt edges.

"A book of unusual merit. The story is exceedingly well told, and the characters are drawn with a freedom and boldness seldom met with."—*Church of England Quarterly.*

"The Irish scenes are of an excellence that has not been surpassed since the best days of Miss Edgeworth."—*Fraser's Magazine.*

WORKS BY THE LATE MRS. R. LEE.

ANECDOTES OF THE HABITS AND INSTINCTS OF
ANIMALS. Third and Cheaper Edition. With Six Illustrations by Weir. Fcap. 8vo, 3s. 6d. cloth, 4s. gilt edges.

ANECDOTES OF THE HABITS AND INSTINCTS OF
BIRDS, FISHES, AND REPTILES. Second and Cheaper
Edition. With Six Illustrations by Harrison Weir. Fcap.
8vo, 3s. 6d. cloth; 4s. gilt edges.

"Amusing, instructive, and ably written."—*Literary Gazette.*
"Mrs. Lee's authorities—to name only one, Professor Owen—are, for
the most part, first-rate."—*Athenæum.*

ADVENTURES IN AUSTRALIA;
Or, The Wanderings of Captain Spencer in the Bush
and the Wilds. Second Edition. Illustrated by Prout.
Fcap. 8vo, 5s. cloth; 5s. 6d. gilt edges.

"This volume should find a place in every school library, and it will, we
are sure, be a very welcome and useful prize."—*Educational Times.*

THE AFRICAN WANDERERS;
Or, The Adventures of Carlos and Antonio; embracing
interesting Descriptions of the Manners and Customs of the
Western Tribes. Third Edition. With Eight Engravings.
Fcap. 8vo, 5s. cloth; 5s. 6d. gilt edges.

"In strongly recommending this admirable work to the attention of
young readers, we feel that we are rendering a real service to the cause of
African civilization."—*Patriot.*

TWELVE STORIES OF THE SAYINGS AND DOINGS OF
ANIMALS. With Illustrations by J. W. Archer.
Third Edition, 2s. 6d. cloth; 3s. 6d. coloured, gilt edges.

PLAYING AT SETTLERS;
Or, The Faggot House. Second Edition. Illustrated
by Gilbert. Price 2s. 6d. cloth; 3s. 6d. coloured.

ELEGANT GIFT FOR A LADY.

TREES, PLANTS, AND FLOWERS;
Their Beauties, Uses, and Influences. By Mrs. R. Lee.
With beautiful coloured Illustrations by J. Andrews. 8vo,
price 10s. 6d. cloth elegant, gilt edges.

"The volume is at once useful as a botanical work, and exquisite as the
ornament of a boudoir table."—*Britannia.*
"As full of interest as of beauty."—*Art Journal.*

W. H. G. KINGSTON'S BOOKS FOR BOYS.

With Illustrations, Fcap. 8vo, price 5s. each, cloth ; 5s. 6d. gilt edges.

TRUE BLUE ;

Or, the Life and Adventures of a British Seaman of the Old School.

" There is about all Mr. Kingston's tales a spirit of hopefulness, honesty, and cheery good principle, which makes them most wholesome as well as most interesting reading. This volume would form an appropriate addition to any ship-board library."—*Era*.

WILL WEATHERHELM :

Or, THE YARN OF AN OLD SAILOR ABOUT HIS EARLY LIFE AND ADVENTURES. Illustrated by G. H. THOMAS.

"Overflowing with maritime adventures, and characters graphically described."—*Critic*.

FRED MARKHAM IN RUSSIA ;

Or, THE BOY TRAVELLERS IN THE LAND OF THE CZAR. With Illustrations by R. T. LANDELLS.

" Most admirably does this book unite a capital narrative with the communication of valuable information respecting Russia."—*Nonconformist*.

SALT WATER ;

Or, NEIL D'ARCY'S SEA LIFE AND ADVENTURES (a Book for Boys). With Eight Illustrations by ANELAY.

" With the exception of Captain Marryat, we know of no English author who will compare with Mr. Kingston as a writer of books of nautical adventure."—*Illustrated News*.

MANCO, THE PERUVIAN CHIEF.

With Illustrations by CARL SCHMOLZE.

" A capital book; the story being one of much interest, and presenting a good account of the history and institutions, the customs and manners of the country."—*Literary Gazette*.

MARK SEAWORTH :

A Tale of the Indian Ocean. With Illustrations by J. ABSOLON. Second Edition.

" No more interesting, nor more safe book, can be put into the hands of youth; and to boys especially ' Mark Seaworth' will be a treasure of delight."—*Art Journal*.

PETER THE WHALER :

His Early Life and Adventures in the Arctic Regions. Second Edition. With Illustrations by E. DUNCAN.

" In short, a book which the old may, but which the young must, read when they have once begun it."—*Athenæum*.

NEW AND BEAUTIFUL LIBRARY EDITION.

THE VICAR OF WAKEFIELD:

A Tale. By OLIVER GOLDSMITH. Printed by Whittingham. With Eight Illustrations by J. ABSOLON. Square fcap. 8vo, price 5s. cloth; 7s. half-bound morocco, Roxburghe style; 10s. 6d. antique morocco.

"Mr. Absolon's graphic sketches add greatly to the interest of the volume; altogether, it is as pretty an edition of the 'Vicar' as we have seen. Mrs. Primrose herself would consider it 'well dressed.'"—*Art Journal.*

"A delightful edition of one of the most delightful of works; the fine old type and thick paper make this volume attractive to any lover of books."—*Edinburgh Guardian.*

GOOD IN EVERYTHING;

Or, THE EARLY HISTORY OF GILBERT HARLAND. By MRS. BARWELL, Author of "Little Lessons for Little Learners," &c. Second Edition. With Illustrations by JOHN GILBERT. Royal 16mo, 2s. 6d. cloth; 3s. 6d. coloured, gilt edges.

"The moral of this exquisite little tale will do more good than a thousand set tasks abounding with dry and uninteresting truisms."—*Bell's Messenger.*

DOMESTIC PETS:

Their Habits and Management; with Illustrative Anecdotes. By MRS. LOUDON. With Illustrations by HARRISON WEIR. Second Thousand. Fcap. 8vo, 2s. 6d. cloth.

CONTENTS :—The Dog, Cat, Squirrel, Rabbit, Guinea-Pig, White Mice, the Parrot and other Talking-Birds, Singing-Birds, Doves and Pigeons, Gold and Silver Fish.

"All who study Mrs. Loudon's pages will be able to treat their pets with certainty and wisdom."—*Standard of Freedom.*

TALES OF SCHOOL LIFE.

By AGNES LOUDON, Author of "Tales for Young People." With Illustrations by JOHN ABSOLON. Second Edition. Royal 16mo, 2s. 6d. plain; 3s. 6d. coloured, gilt edges.

"These reminiscences of school-days will be recognised as truthful pictures of every-day occurrence. The style is colloquial and pleasant, and therefore well suited to those for whose perusal it is intended."—*Athenæum.*

THE FAVOURITE LIBRARY.

A Series of Works for the Young; each with an Illustration by a well-known Artist. Price ONE SHILLING, cloth.

1. THE ESKDALE HERD-BOY. By LADY STODDART.

2. MRS. LEICESTER'S SCHOOL. By CHARLES and MARY LAMB.

3. HISTORY OF THE ROBINS. By MRS. TRIMMER.

4. MEMOIRS OF BOB THE SPOTTED TERRIER.

5. KEEPER'S TRAVELS IN SEARCH OF HIS MASTER.

6. THE SCOTTISH ORPHANS. By LADY STODDART.

7. NEVER WRONG; or, THE YOUNG DISPUTANT; and "IT WAS ONLY IN FUN."

8. THE LIFE AND PERAMBULATIONS OF A MOUSE.

9. EASY INTRODUCTION TO THE KNOWLEDGE OF NATURE. By MRS. TRIMMER.

10. RIGHT AND WRONG. By the Author of "Always Happy."

11. HARRY'S HOLIDAY. By JEFFERYS TAYLOR.

12. SHORT POEMS AND HYMNS FOR CHILDREN.

The above may be had, Two Volumes bound in one, at Two Shillings cloth; or 2s. 6d. gilt edges, as follows :—

1. LADY STODDART'S SCOTTISH TALES.

2. ANIMAL HISTORIES. THE DOG.

3. ANIMAL HISTORIES. THE ROBINS and MOUSE.

4. TALES FOR BOYS. HARRY'S HOLIDAY and NEVER WRONG.

5. TALES FOR GIRLS. MRS. LEICESTER'S SCHOOL and RIGHT AND WRONG.

6. POETRY AND NATURE. SHORT POEMS and TRIMMER'S INTRODUCTION.

TALES FROM CATLAND.

Dedicated to the Young Kittens of England. By an OLD TABBY. Illustrated by H. WEIR. Fourth Edition. Small 4to, 2s. 6d. plain; 3s. 6d. coloured.

"The combination of quiet humour and sound sense has made this one of the pleasantest little books of the season."—*Lady's Newspaper.*

THE WONDERS OF HOME, IN ELEVEN STORIES.

By GRANDFATHER GREY. With Illustrations. Third Edition, roy. 16mo, 2s. 6d. cloth; 3s. 6d. coloured.—*Contents :—*

Story of—1. A CUP OF TEA. 2. A PIECE OF SUGAR.
   3. A MILK-JUG. 4. A LUMP OF COAL.
   5. SOME HOT WATER. 6. A PIN.
   7. JENNY'S SASH. 8. HARRY'S JACKET.
   9. A TUMBLER. 10. A KNIFE.
    11. THIS BOOK.

"The idea is excellent, and its execution equally commendable. The subjects are very happily told in a light yet sensible manner."—*Weekly News.*

EVERY-DAY THINGS;

Or, USEFUL KNOWLEDGE respecting the PRINCIPAL ANIMAL, VEGETABLE, and MINERAL SUBSTANCES in COMMON USE. Written for Young Persons, by a LADY. Second Edition, revised. 18mo, 1s. 6d. cloth.

"A little encyclopædia of useful knowledge; deserving a place in every juvenile library."—*Evangelical Magazine.*

PRICE SIXPENCE EACH, PLAIN; ONE SHILLING, COLOURED.

In super-royal 16mo, beautifully printed, each with Seven Illustrations by HARRISON WEIR, *and Descriptions by* MRS. LEE.

  1. BRITISH ANIMALS. First Series.
  2. BRITISH ANIMALS. Second Series.
  3. BRITISH BIRDS.
  4. FOREIGN ANIMALS. First Series.
  5. FOREIGN ANIMALS. Second Series.
  6. FOREIGN BIRDS.

. Or bound in One Vol. under the title of "Familiar Natural History," *see page* 19.

Uniform in size and price with the above.

THE FARM AND ITS SCENES. With Six Pictures from Drawings by HARRISON WEIR.

THE DIVERTING HISTORY OF JOHN GILPIN. With Six Illustrations by WATTS PHILLIPS.

THE PEACOCK AT HOME AND THE BUTTERFLY'S BALL. With Four Illustrations by HARRISON WEIR.

A WORD TO THE WISE;

Or, HINTS ON THE CURRENT IMPROPRIETY OF EXPRESSION IN WRITING AND SPEAKING. By PARRY GWYNNE. Tenth Thousand. 18mo, price 6d. sewed, or 1s. cloth, gilt edges.

"All who wish to mind their p's and q's should consult this little volume."—*Gentleman's Magazine.*

"May be advantageously consulted by even the well-educated."—*Athenæum.*

STORIES OF JULIAN AND HIS PLAYFELLOWS.

Written by his Mamma. With Four Illustrations by JOHN ABSOLON. Second Edition. Small 4to, 2s. 6d. plain; 3s. 6d. coloured, gilt edges.

"The lessons taught by Julian's mamma are each fraught with an excellent moral."—*Morning Advertiser.*

BLADES AND FLOWERS;

Poems for Children. By M. S. C. Frontispiece by H. ANELAY. Fcap. 8vo, price 2s. cloth.

"Breathing the same spirit as the nursery poems of Jane Taylor."—*Literary Gazette.*

AUNT JANE'S VERSES FOR CHILDREN.

By Mrs. T. D. CREWDSON. Illustrated with twelve beautiful Engravings. Fcap. 8vo, 3s. 6d. cloth.

"A charming little volume of excellent moral and religious tendency."—*Evangelical Magazine.*

ILLUSTRATED BY GEORGE CRUIKSHANK.

KIT BAM, THE BRITISH SINBAD;

Or, THE YARNS OF AN OLD MARINER. By MARY COWDEN CLARKE, Author of "The Concordance to Shakspeare," &c. Fcap. 8vo, price 3s. 6d. cloth; 4s. gilt edges.

"A more captivating volume for juvenile recreative reading we never remember to have seen."—*Standard of Freedom.*

RHYMES OF ROYALTY.

THE HISTORY OF ENGLAND in Verse, from the Norman Conquest to the reign of QUEEN VICTORIA; with an Appendix, comprising a Summary of the leading events in each reign. Fcap. 8vo, with Frontispiece. 2s. 6d. cloth.

THE LADY'S ALBUM OF FANCY WORK;

Consisting of Novel, Elegant, and Useful Patterns in Knitting, Netting, Crochet, and Embroidery, printed in colours. Bound in a beautiful cover. New Edit. Post 4to, 3s. 6d. gilt edges.

VISITS TO BEECHWOOD FARM;

Or, COUNTRY PLEASURES AND HINTS FOR HAPPINESS, ADDRESSED TO THE YOUNG. By CATHARINE M. A. COUPER. Illustrations by ABSOLON. Small 4to, 3s. 6d. plain; 4s. 6d. col.

" The work is well calculated to impress upon the minds of the young the superiority of simple and natural pleasures over those which are artificial."
—*Englishwoman's Magazine.*

MARIN DE LA VOYE'S ELEMENTARY FRENCH WORKS.

LES JEUNES NARRATEURS;

Ou, PETITS CONTES MORAUX. With a Key to the difficult Words and Phrases. Frontispiece. Second Edition. 18mo, 2s. cloth.

" Written in pure and easy French."—*Morning Post.*

THE PICTORIAL FRENCH GRAMMAR,

FOR THE USE OF CHILDREN. With Eighty Engravings. Royal 16mo ; price 1s. 6d. cloth; 1s. sewed.

" The publication has greater than mechanical merit; it contains the principal elements of the French language, exhibited in a plain and expressive manner."—*Spectator.*

THE FIRST BOOK OF GEOGRAPHY:

A Text Book for Beginners, and a Guide to the Young Teacher. By HUGO REID, Author of "Elements of Astronomy." Third Edition, carefully revised. 18mo, 1s. sewed.

"One of the most sensible little books on the subject of Geography we have met with."—*Educational Times.* "As a lesson-book it will charm the pupil by its brief, natural style."—*Episcopalian.*

THE MODERN BRITISH PLUTARCH;

Or, LIVES OF MEN DISTINGUISHED IN THE RECENT HISTORY OF OUR COUNTRY FOR THEIR TALENTS, VIRTUES, AND ACHIEVEMENTS. By W. C. TAYLOR, LL.D., Author of "A Manual of Ancient and Modern History," &c. 12mo. Second Thousand. 4s. 6d. cloth; 5s. gilt edges.

"A work which will be welcomed in any circle of intelligent young persons."—*British Quarterly Review.*

HOME AMUSEMENTS:

A Choice Collection of Riddles, Charades, Conundrums, Parlour Games, and Forfeits. By PETER PUZZLEWELL, Esq., of Rebus Hall. New Edition, revised and enlarged, with Frontispiece by H. K. BROWNE (Phiz). 16mo, 2s. 6d. cloth.

EARLY DAYS OF ENGLISH PRINCES.

By MRS. RUSSELL GREY. Dedicated, by permission, to the Duchess of Roxburghe. With Illustrations by JOHN FRANKLIN. Small 4to, 3s. 6d. cloth; 4s. 6d. coloured, gilt edges.

"Just the book for giving children some first notions of English history, as the personages it speaks about are themselves young."—*Manchester Examiner.*

FIRST STEPS TO SCOTTISH HISTORY.

By MISS RODWELL, Author of "First Steps to English History." With Ten Illustrations by WEIGALL. 16mo, 3s. 6d. cloth; 4s. 6d. coloured.

"It is the first popular book in which we have seen the outlines of the early history of the Scottish tribes exhibited with anything like accuracy."—*Glasgow Constitutional.*

"The work is throughout agreeably and lucidly written."—*Midland Counties Herald.*

LONDON CRIES AND PUBLIC EDIFICES,

Illustrated in Twenty-four Engravings by LUKE LIMNER;
with descriptive Letter-press. Square 12mo, 2s. 6d. plain;
5s. coloured. Bound in emblematic cover.

THE CELESTIAL EMPIRE;

Or, POINTS AND PICKINGS OF INFORMATION ABOUT CHINA
AND THE CHINESE. By the late "OLD HUMPHREY." With
Twenty Engravings. Fcap. 8vo, 3s. 6d. cloth; 4s. gilt edges.

"The book is exactly what the author proposed it should be, full of good
information, good feeling, and good temper."—*Allen's Indian Mail.*

"Even well-known topics are treated with a graceful air of novelty."—
Athenæum.

TALES FROM THE COURT OF OBERON:

Containing the favourite Histories of TOM THUMB, GRACIOSA
AND PERCINET, VALENTINE AND ORSON, and CHILDREN IN
THE WOOD. With Sixteen Illustrations by ALFRED CROW-
QUILL. Small 4to, 2s. 6d. plain; 3s. 6d. coloured.

GLIMPSES OF NATURE,

AND OBJECTS OF INTEREST DESCRIBED, DURING A VISIT TO
THE ISLE OF WIGHT. Designed to assist and encourage
Young Persons in forming habits of Observation. By MRS.
LOUDON. Second Edition, enlarged. With Forty-one Illus-
trations. 3s. 6d. cloth.

"We could not recommend a more valuable little volume. It is full of
information, conveyed in the most agreeable manner."—*Literary Gazette.*

THE SILVER SWAN:

A Fairy Tale. By MADAME DE CHATELAIN. Illustrated by
JOHN LEECH. Small 4to, 2s. 6d. plain; 3s. 6d. coloured cloth.

"The moral is in the good, broad, unmistakeable style of the best fairy
period."—*Athenæum.*

"The story is written with excellent taste and sly humour."—*Atlas.*

WORKS BY THE AUTHOR OF MAMMA'S BIBLE STORIES.

FANNY AND HER MAMMA;

Or, EASY LESSONS FOR CHILDREN. In which it is attempted to bring Scriptural Principles into Daily Practice. Illustrated by J. GILBERT. Third Edition. 16mo, 2s. 6d. cloth ; 3s. 6d. coloured, gilt edges.

"A little book in beautiful large clear type, to suit the capacity of infant readers, which we can with pleasure recommend."—*Christian Lady's Mag.*

SHORT AND SIMPLE PRAYERS

FOR THE USE OF YOUNG CHILDREN, WITH HYMNS. Fifth Edition. Square 16mo, 1s. 6d. cloth.

"Well adapted to the capacities of children,—beginning with the simplest forms which the youngest child may lisp at its mother's knee, and proceeding with those suited to its gradually advancing age. Special prayers, designed for particular circumstances and occasions, are added. We cordially recommend the book."—*Christian Guardian.*

MAMMA'S BIBLE STORIES

FOR HER LITTLE BOYS AND GIRLS, adapted to the capacities of very young children. Eleventh Edition, with Twelve Engravings. 2s. 6d. cloth ; 3s. 6d. coloured, gilt edges.

A SEQUEL TO MAMMA'S BIBLE STORIES.

Fifth and Cheaper Edition. With Twelve Illustrations. 2s. 6d. cloth ; 3s. 6d. coloured, gilt edges.

SCRIPTURE HISTORIES FOR LITTLE CHILDREN.

With Sixteen Illustrations by JOHN GILBERT. Super-royal 16mo, price 3s. cloth ; 4s. 6d. coloured, gilt edges.

CONTENTS:

The History of Joseph.	History of our Saviour.
History of Moses.	The Miracles of Christ.

*** *Sold separately: 6d. each, plain ; 1s. coloured.*

BIBLE SCENES;

Or, SUNDAY EMPLOYMENT FOR VERY YOUNG CHILDREN. Consisting of Twelve Coloured Illustrations on Cards, and the History written in Simple Language. In a neat Box, 3s. 6d.; or dissected as a Puzzle, 6s. 6d.

First Series: History of Joseph.	Third Series: History of Moses.
Second Series : History of our Saviour.	Fourth Series : The Miracles of Christ.

"It is hoped that these 'Scenes' may form a useful and interesting addition to the Sabbath occupations of the Nursery. From their very earliest infancy little children will listen with interest and delight to stories brought thus palpably before their eyes by means of illustration."—*Preface.*

RHODA;

Or, THE EXCELLENCE OF CHARITY. Fourth Edition. With Illustrations. 16mo, 2s. cloth.

"Not only adapted for children, but many parents might derive great advantage from studying its simple truths."—*Church and State Gazette.*

TRUE STORIES FROM ANCIENT HISTORY,

Chronologically arranged from the Creation of the World to the Death of Charlemagne. Twelfth Edition. With 24 Steel Engravings. 12mo, 5s. cloth.

TRUE STORIES FROM MODERN HISTORY,

Chronologically arranged from the Death of Charlemagne to the Present Time. Eighth Edition. With 24 Steel Engravings. 12mo, 5s. cloth.

MRS. TRIMMER'S HISTORY OF ENGLAND.

Revised and brought down to the Present Time by Mrs. MILNER. With Portraits of the Sovereigns in their proper costume, and Frontispiece by HARVEY. New Edition in One Volume. 5s. cloth.

"The editing has been very judiciously done. The work has an established reputation for the clearness of its genealogical and chronological tables, and for its pervading tone of Christian piety."—*Church and State Gazette.*

STORIES FROM THE OLD AND NEW TESTAMENTS,

On an improved plan. By the Rev. BOURNE HALL DRAPER. With 48 Engravings. Sixth Edition. 12mo, 5s. cloth.

THE WARS OF THE JEWS,

As related by JOSEPHUS; adapted to the capacities of Young Persons. With 24 Engravings. Sixth Edit. 4s. 6d. cloth.

THE PRINCE OF WALES'S PRIMER.

With 300 Illustrations by J. GILBERT. Dedicated to Her Majesty. New Edition, price 6d.; with title and cover printed in gold and colours, 1s.

HOW TO BE HAPPY;

Or, FAIRY GIFTS: to which is added, A SELECTION OF MORAL ALLEGORIES, from the best English Writers. Second Edition. With 8 Engravings. 12mo, 3s. 6d. cloth.

THE ABBE GAULTIER'S GEOGRAPHICAL WORKS.

I. FAMILIAR GEOGRAPHY,

With a concise Treatise on the Artificial Sphere, and two coloured Maps, illustrative of the principal Geographical Terms. Fifteenth Edition. 16mo, 3s. cloth.

II. AN ATLAS,

Adapted to the Abbé Gaultier's Geographical Games, consisting of 8 Maps, coloured, and 7 in Outline, &c. Folio, 15s. half-bound.

BUTLER'S OUTLINE MAPS, AND KEY;

Or, Geographical and Biographical Exercises; with a Set of Coloured Outline Maps; designed for the Use of Young Persons. By the late WILLIAM BUTLER. Enlarged by the Author's Son, J. O. BUTLER. Thirty-second Edition, revised. Price 4s.

BATTLE-FIELDS.

A graphic Guide to the Places described in the History of England as the scenes of such Events; with the situation of the principal Naval Engagements fought on the Coast of the British Empire. By Mr. WAUTHIER, Geographer. On a large sheet, 3s. 6d.; in case, 6s.; or mounted on rollers, varnished, 9s.

TABULAR VIEWS OF THE GEOGRAPHY AND SACRED HISTORY OF PALESTINE, & OF THE TRAVELS OF ST. PAUL. Intended for Pupil Teachers, and others engaged in Class Teaching. By A. T. WHITE. Oblong 8vo, price 1s. sewed.

THE CHILD'S GRAMMAR.

By the late Lady FENN, under the assumed name of Mrs. Lovechild. Forty-ninth Edition. 18mo, 9d. cloth.

ROWBOTHAM'S NEW AND EASY METHOD OF LEARNING the FRENCH GENDERS. New Edition. 6d.

BELLENGER'S FRENCH WORD AND PHRASE-BOOK;

Containing a select Vocabulary and Dialogues, for the Use of Beginners. New Edition, 1s. sewed.

DER SCHWÄTZER;

Or, THE PRATTLER. An amusing Introduction to the German Language, on the Plan of "Le Babillard." With 16 Illustrations. Price 2s. cloth.

ALWAYS HAPPY;

Or, Anecdotes of Felix and his Sister Serena. By the Author of "Claudine," &c. Eighteenth Edition, with new Illustrations. Royal 18mo, price 2s. 6d. cloth.

ANDERSEN'S (H. C.) NIGHTINGALE AND OTHER TALES.

2s. 6d. plain ; 3s. 6d. coloured.

ANECDOTES OF KINGS,

Selected from History ; or, Gertrude's Stories for Children. New Edition. With Engravings. 2s. 6d. plain ; 3s. 6d. coloured.

BIBLE ILLUSTRATIONS;

Or, a Description of Manners and Customs peculiar to the East. By the Rev. B. H. DRAPER. With Engravings. Fourth Edition. Revised by DR. KITTO. 3s. 6d. cloth.

THE BRITISH HISTORY BRIEFLY TOLD,

And a Description of the Ancient Customs, Sports, and Pastimes of the English. Embellished with full-length Portraits of the Sovereigns of England in their proper Costumes, and 18 other Engravings. 3s. 6d. cloth.

CHIT-CHAT;

Or, Short Tales in Short Words. By a MOTHER, Author of "Always Happy." Eighth Edition. With New Engravings. 2s. 6d. cloth ; 3s. 6d. coloured, gilt edges.

CONVERSATIONS ON THE LIFE OF JESUS CHRIST,

For the Use of Children. By a MOTHER. A New Edition. With 12 Engravings. 2s. 6d. plain ; 3s. 6d. coloured.

COSMORAMA.

The Manners, Customs, and Costumes of all Nations of the World described. By J. ASPIN. New Edition, with numerous Illustrations. 3s. 6d. plain ; and 4s. 6d. coloured.

INFANTINE KNOWLEDGE;

A Spelling and Reading Book, on a Popular Plan, combining much Useful Information with the Rudiments of Learning. By the Author of "The Child's Grammar." With numerous Engravings. Ninth Edit. 2s. 6d. plain ; 3s. 6d. col.

FACTS TO CORRECT FANCIES;

Or, Short Narratives compiled from the Biography of Remarkable Women. By a MOTHER. With Engravings. 3s. 6d. plain ; 4s. 6d. coloured.

FRUITS OF ENTERPRISE,

Exhibited in the Travels of Belzoni in Egypt and Nubia. Thirteenth Edition, with six Illustrations by BIRKET FOSTER. 18mo, price 3s. cloth.

THE GARDEN;

Or, Frederick's Monthly Instructions for the Management and Formation of a Flower-Garden. Fourth Edition. With Engravings of the Flowers in Bloom for each Month in the Year, &c. 3s. 6d. plain ; or 6s. with the Flowers col.

EASY LESSONS;

Or, Leading-Strings to Knowledge. New Edition, with 8 Engravings. 2s. 6d. plain ; 3s. 6d. coloured.

KEY TO KNOWLEDGE ;

Or, Things in Common Use simply and shortly explained. By a MOTHER, Author of " Always Happy," &c. Thirteenth Edition. With Sixty Illustrations. 3s. 6d. cloth.

THE LADDER TO LEARNING :

A Collection of Fables, Original and Select, arranged progressively in words of One, Two, and Three Syllables. Edited and improved by the late MRS. TRIMMER. With 79 Cuts. Nineteenth Edition. 3s. 6d. cloth.

LITTLE LESSONS FOR LITTLE LEARNERS,

In Words of One Syllable. By MRS. BARWELL. Ninth Edit., with numerous Illustrations. 2s. 6d. plain; 3s. 6d. col.

THE LITTLE READER;

A Progressive Step to Knowledge. Fourth Edition, with sixteen Plates. Price 2s. 6d. cloth.

MAMMA'S LESSONS

For her Little Boys and Girls. Thirteenth Edition, with eight Engravings. Price 2s. 6d. cloth ; 3s. 6d. coloured, gilt edges.

THE MINE ;

Or, Subterranean Wonders. An Account of the Operations of the Miner, and the Products of his Labours. By the late Rev. ISAAC TAYLOR. Sixth Edition, with numerous corrections and additions, by Mrs. LOUDON. With 45 Woodcuts and 16 Steel Engravings. 3s. 6d. cloth.

THE OCEAN:

A Description of Wonders and important Products of the Sea. Second Edition. With Illustrations of 37 Genera of Shells, by SOWERBY; and 4 Steel and 50 Wood Engravings. 3s. 6d. cloth.

THE RIVAL CRUSOES,

And other Tales. By AGNES STRICKLAND, Author of "The Queens of England." Sixth Edition. Price 2s. 6d. cloth.

SHORT TALES,

Written for Children. By DAME TRUELOVE and her Friends. A new Edition, with 20 Engravings. 3s. 6d. cloth.

THE STUDENTS;

Or, Biographies of the Grecian Philosophers. 12mo, price 2s. 6d. cloth.

STORIES OF EDWARD AND HIS LITTLE FRIENDS.

With 12 Illustrations. Second Edit. 3s. 6d. plain ; 4s. 6d. col.

SUNDAY LESSONS FOR LITTLE CHILDREN.

By Mrs. BARWELL. Fourth Edition. 2s. 6d. plain ; 3s. col.

A VISIT TO GROVE COTTAGE,

And the India Cabinet Opened. By the Author of "Fruits of Enterprise." New Edition. 18mo, price 3s. cloth.

DISSECTIONS FOR YOUNG CHILDREN.

In a Neat Box. Price 5s. each.

1. Scenes from the Lives of Joseph and Moses.
2. Scenes from the History of Our Saviour.
3. Old Mother Hubbard and her Dog.
4. The Life and Death of Cock Robin.

TWO SHILLINGS EACH, CLOTH.

With Frontispiece, &c.

DER SCHWÄTZER: an amusing Introduction to the German Language. 16 plates.

LE BABILLARD; an amusing Introduction to the French Language. 16 plates. Sixth Edition.

COUNSELS AT HOME; with Anecdotes, Tales, &c.

MORAL TALES. By a Father. With 2 Engravings.

ANECDOTES OF PETER THE GREAT, Emperor of Russia. 18mo.

ONE SHILLING AND SIXPENCE EACH, CLOTH.

THE DAUGHTER OF A GENIUS. By MRS. HOFLAND.

ELLEN THE TEACHER. By MRS. HOFLAND.

THE SON OF A GENIUS. By MRS. HOFLAND.

THEODORE ; or, the Crusaders. By MRS. HOFLAND.

TRIMMER'S (MRS.) OLD TESTAMENT LESSONS. With 40 Engravings.

TRIMMER'S (MRS.) NEW TESTAMENT LESSONS. With 40 Engravings.

ONE SHILLING EACH, CLOTH.

SPRING FLOWERS and the MONTHLY MONITOR.

THE CHILD'S DUTY.

THE HISTORY OF PRINCE LEE BOO. Twentieth Edition.

Price 1s. plain, 1s. 6d. coloured cloth.

THE DAISY. Twenty-seventh Edition. With Thirty Engravings.

THE COWSLIP. Twenty-fourth Edition. With Thirty Engravings.

DURABLE NURSERY BOOKS,

MOUNTED ON CLOTH, WITH COLOURED PLATES,

ONE SHILLING EACH.

1 Alphabet of Goody Two-Shoes.
2 Cinderella.
3 Cock Robin.
4 Courtship of Jenny Wren.
5 Dame Trot and her Cat.
6 History of an Apple Pie.
7 House that Jack built.
8 Little Rhymes for Little Folks.
9 Mother Hubbard.
10 Monkey's Frolic.
11 Old Woman and her Pig.
12 Puss in Boots.
13 Tommy Trip's Museum of Birds, Part I.
14 ——————— Part II.

DURABLE BOOKS FOR SUNDAY READING.

Price 6d. each.

SCENES FROM THE LIVES OF JOSEPH AND MOSES. With Illustrations by JOHN GILBERT. Printed on Linen.

SCENES FROM THE HISTORY OF OUR SAVIOUR. With Illustrations by JOHN GILBERT. Printed on Linen.

ONE THOUSAND ARITHMETICAL TESTS ;

Or, the Examiner's Assistant, specially adapted, by a Novel Arrangement of the Subject, for Examination Purposes, but also suited for general Use in Schools. By T. S. CAYZER, Head Master of Queen Elizabeth's Hospital, Bristol. Second Edition, revised and stereotyped. 12mo, price 1s. 6d. cloth.

Answers to the above, price 1s. 6d. cloth.

DARNELL'S EDUCATIONAL WORKS.

The attention of all interested in the subject of Education is invited to these Works, now in extensive use throughout the Kingdom, prepared by Mr. DARNELL, a Schoolmaster of many years' experience.

1. COPY BOOKS.—A SURE AND CERTAIN ROAD TO A GOOD HANDWRITING, gradually advancing from the Simple Stroke to a superior Small-hand.

LARGE POST, Sixteen Numbers, 6d. each.

FOOLSCAP, Twenty Numbers, to which are added three Supplementary Numbers of Angular Writing for Ladies, and one of Ornamental Hands. Price 3d. each.

*** This series may also be had on very superior paper, marble covers, 4d. each.

"For teaching writing I would recommend the use of Darnell's Copy Books. I have noticed a marked improvement wherever they have been used."—*Report of Mr. Mayo (National School Organizer of Schools) to the Worcester Diocesan Board of Education.*

2. GRAMMAR made intelligible to Children, 1s. cloth.

3. ARITHMETIC made intelligible to Children, 1s. 6d. cloth.

.*.* Key to Parts 2 and 3, price 1s. cloth.

4. READING, a Short and Certain Road to, price 6d. cloth.

GRIFFITH AND FARRAN,

CORNER OF ST. PAUL'S CHURCHYARD.

www.ingramcontent.com/pod-product-compliance
Lightning Source LLC
Chambersburg PA
CBHW030110030726
47498CB00007B/2324